FAMILY REUNION

FAMILY REUNION

Story by **KENNON A. KEITH**

ReadersMagnet, LLC

Natalie Cordova sits in the waiting room of Mystique Models Management, waiting anxiously to meet with the lead photographer, Jean-Philippe Aristide. He is one of France's most respected photographers, a talent scout for the agency, as well as owner. If Natalie could impress him, she would be assured of a contract. She would accomplish what her Nana taught her she was born to do. As she sits in silent anticipation, she takes the time to reflect on her life.

One year ago, she was at her lowest point. She was harassed, tormented, and taunted by bullies every day. She was a pacifist, so she never knew how to stop it. She felt fear, sorrow, and rage for everyday of her 18 years of life. She was a family outcast; not even her own mother would put up with her, and she was given to her grandmother when she was 12 years old. All her feelings came to a head exactly one year ago.

She was savagely beaten and knocked unconscious. As she lay on the ground, beaten and bloodied, she made the decision that would change her life. She changed her outlook from sorrow and pity, into rage and revenge. She transformed who she was to the point of non-recognition. Her body, attitude, and mind evolved from pacifist, to murderous. By her hand, seven people were executed, and by her actions, 24 more perished as well. After her return home six months ago, she felt she had to change paths in life. She would seize her family heritage, and once she reached the pinnacle, she would shun those she felt deserved no joy in her success, namely her Nana Rebecca, and her mother Raylene.

Unfortunately, her family heritage is in the modeling business, and she is having great difficulty getting her foot in the door for international work. Her resume is weak, including only small shots in a couple of women's magazines over the past six months. Her Nana has been on the phone, booking jobs and auditions, and Natalie has traversed the Western United States trying to make a positive impression on the industry. Many photographers have called back with more work, but these were not the opportunities that Nana was looking for.

A break came four days ago, when Mr. Aristide called personally, wanting to shoot Natalie for a potential contract with his agency, Mystique Models Management. This agency is the premier agency in the Pacific Northwest United States, with many international contacts. Aristide had gotten a hold of Natalie's portfolio and thought she had potential. He called and scheduled a shoot at his Portland studio.

Natalie's cell phone rings and brings her back to reality. She checks the caller I.D. and recognizes Nana's cell number. She answers the phone.

"Hi Nana." She says.

"How'd it go?" Rebecca asks.

"It hasn't happened yet." Natalie replies. "He's still not here."

"What?!" Nana shouts. "He promised me! Where the fuck is he?"

"Calm down Nana." Natalie replies. "This is too important, and I can't afford to rush him."

"I swear," Nana continued, "if he flakes on you, I'll drive your truck right up his ass!"

"Don't know if you should." Natalie remarks, "He might like it."

Both women share a good laugh.

"Alright." Nana answers. "You call me as soon as you're done."

"No problem." Natalie responds. "Talk to you later."

"Bye-bye my dear." Rebecca says and hangs up the phone.

Pushy wrinkled bitch!

Natalie hangs up the phone and sulks in her seat. She always hated how demanding Nana was, and wishes there was some way to mellow her out. She clears her mind and watches the television in the waiting room. The receptionist had informed her earlier that they have a satellite system, so she decided to watch TV while she waited. She checked the guide and turned to the Style Channel. She caught the middle of a program called "Limelight, and the City of Angels." It's a program about the celebrity lifestyles in Los Angeles, California. On the program, Natalie watches an interview between the show's host and Los Angeles area top model, Willow Carter.

The interview catches Natalie by surprise. Willow is covered in tattoos. Her arms, legs, and back are covered, plus she has at least three on her neck and one on her face. Along with her tattoos, she has three rings in each ear, one in her nose, one in her bottom lip, three in her tongue, and one in each eyebrow. She talks about how she manages her modeling career with her punk lifestyle, and her language is very profane. Her refers to her co-workers as her bitches and drops f-bombs with ever other sentence. She revels that she was brought into modeling less than a year ago because of her eyes, and Natalie could see why. They were big and a deep aqua blue in color. When she stood up and posed for the host, she showed off her perfect body, complete with six-pack abs and buns of steel.

The program is very interesting and Natalie pays close attention. The segment is almost complete when the waiting room doors opens, and a man in his early to mid 40's walks in. He sees Natalie, smiles and scuttles over to her.

"Mademoiselle Cordova n'est pas?" He asks.

"Oui." She replies as she stands.

"Bonne!" He responds. "Je m'appelle Jean-Philippe Astride. Comment t'allez vous aujord'hui?"

"Je vais tres bien, merci." She replies. "Et vous?"

"Tres bien aussi" He answers. "Je suis si heureux de vous rencontrer! Vous êtes aussi belles que vous la grand-mère a promis."

Natalie politely shakes his hand and tries not to let on that she has no idea what he just said. He takes her hand and kisses it lightly. He looks at her and waits for a response. She does not want to be rude, so she responds quickly.

"Um… thank you." She says. "Thank you so much." She gives a quiet chuckle.

"Ah," he responds, "so zee truth comes out no?"

"I'm sorry." She replies. "I just started learning French."

"Oh, no vorries." He says. "I appreciate zee effort. Come, let me look at you darling."

He motions for her to join him inside the studio. She stands in the center of the set, and he walks around her, making nice little comments as he checks her out.

"Very nice my dear." He says. "I do not know what it is vith you American girls, but you has such vonderful shape and bone structure, yeah?"

"Thank you." Natalie answers. "Must be something in the water."

"Well, let us hope so and thank God for zat." He replies. "Now, vhat is it zat you should vant me to see you in?"

"I leave that to your discretion." She answers. "Your eyes know better than mine."

"Say no more my dear." He responds. "I vant to see you draped in silk, and soft vhite. Fabrice!"

He calls out for his assistant. A young man in his twenties runs over with a flamboyant strut and stands at full attention before his boss.

"Fabrice," he continues, "I vant you to give zis angel her vings. Silk in soft vhite, please do crimp zee locks, pout zee luscious lips, and focus on zee curves."

"Oui, pas de probleme." Fabrice answers. He takes Natalie by the hand and begins to lead her away.

"Et Fabrice," Aristide calls out, "je veux son chic, svelte et sexy. Je veux plus d'adonis et moins de salope. Allez maintenant!"

"Comme vous voulez." Fabrice responds. "Venez avec moi mon amour."

Natalie follows Fabrice to the back changing room. Once inside, Natalie sees other girls getting prepared for separate shoots. Some girls were getting makeup nude while their clothes were being prepped; others were fully clothed and getting finishing touches. All the girls were very catty. Natalie encountered stares and dirty looks while following Fabrice to a clothing rack. Once at the rack, Fabrice speaks in broken English.

"White. Silken. Teddy." He stammers.

He pulls out some white lingerie and undergarment, hands them to Natalie and points to a dressing room.

"You change." He says. "Five minutes. Station seven."

He points to an empty makeup station.

"Okay." Natalie replies.

She takes the garments and heads into the dressing room. Once the door is locked, she strips naked and puts on the lingerie. She examines herself in the mirror and is pretty pleased. The material is soft and feels smooth on her skin. It squeezes her breast and accentuates her cleavage. Her shapely backside is outlined by the delicate fabric and the silk panties feel wonderful between her legs. She is most pleased however, that the piece is not see-through, and the tattoo on her back is well hidden.

Emerging from the dressing room, she heads for the aforementioned makeup station. Once there, she is surrounded by various people. A man stands in front of her and begins to apply her makeup, a woman stands behind her begins to style her hair, and two other woman begin quick work on her hands and feet. After 45 minutes in the chair, she is done, and led to her set by her makeup artist. On the set, she reunites with Jean-Philippe.

"Zere she is!" He exclaims. "Zere is zee angel."

Natalie smiles as they kiss each other's cheeks.

"Okay my darling." He continues. "Zis is Anya Juneau. She is my protégé, and will do zee snapping of zee photos."

He motions to a woman holding a camera, who waves at Natalie.

"I was under the impression," Natalie remarks, "that you were taking the shots."

"Alas, mon amoure," he replies, "I have seen all zat I must see. I will be on set to direct zee shoot. I promise you, if zee camera loves you, only half as much as I love you; and believe me I do love you, zen you are set, and I believe zat it vill."

Comforted, Natalie goes to the center of the set and begins to pose. Anya begins taking the shots, and Jean-Philippe begins to give direction. He does not make many suggestions, as he is adamant, that Natalie is doing great. With each new pose, he showers more praise onto her. After one hour, he demands that they continue, saying he is so pleased he does not want to stop. Ninety minutes pass before the session ends. At the conclusion, he runs up to Natalie and gives her a big kiss on the cheek. She gives him a hug in return and gives one to Anya as well.

" Vous êtes une vision mon cher!" He says. "You are a vision, a true vision. Miss Rebecca spoke true about you. Tell her she is in my heart, and I vill contact zee both of you so very soon."

"Merci beaucoup Jean-Philippe." Natalie replies. "I truly appreciate your words."

"Please, no, zee pleasure is mine and I vill savor every morsel of it." He answers before he takes his leave.

Natalie gives him a friendly wave as he walks away and gives one last thank you to Anya. She returns to her dressing room and changes back into her regular clothes. She neatly arranges the lingerie on their hanger and prepares to return them to the rack. As she leaves the dressing room she is confronted by a young lady, roughly her age and height, but with dark brown tresses and smaller breasts.

"Hey there vision!" She says sarcastically and chuckles. Natalie does not like her tone.

"What do you want?" Natalie asks.

"Wow." The girl continues. "You really are a rookie. You don't even know the language."

"What the hell are you talking about?" She asks, getting angry.

"He called you a vision." The girl says says. "A vision, as in seen it before, and don't care to see it again. You're done bitch."

The girl laughs to herself as she backs away. While she is stepping back, Natalie can see what she is wearing. Blue jeans and a pink shirt with the name Lynn spelled out in sequins.

LYNN!

Natalie's mind flashes back to her previous encounter with a Lynn, Lynn Bennett, the girl Natalie strangled and corpse she planted for Heather to find. Natalie felt her anger build, and turn to rage. As the girl turns to walk away, Natalie smiles and calls out to her.

"Hey, uh, Lynn is it?" Natalie asks.

The girl turns back around.

"Oh," she says, "you can read? I'm shocked."

"Yeah, I can read." Natalie answers. "You know what else I can do?"

"No," the girl answers. "and I really don't give a fu..."

WHAM!

Natalie rears back and punches the girl in the nose, sending her sprawling to the ground. The girl lands hard on her backside and smacks her head on the floor. Natalie jumps on top of her and presses her knee into the girl's neck, cutting off her air supply. While the girl struggles to breathe, Natalie reaches down and squeezes her victim's nose between her index and middle fingers. With a quick torque of her wrist, she twists and snaps the girl's nose, breaking it at the bridge. She tries to shriek in pain but can get no air through her constricted throat. Natalie presses her knee harder and leans in close to the close to the girl's ear.

"I can do," she whispers, "and have done, a whole lot worse!"

The girl squirms as she uses one hand to try and fight off Natalie, and the other to stop her bleeding nose. After a minute, she loses her air, blacks out, and loses consciousness. Natalie gets off the girl, grabs her by the hair, and dumps her into a nearby closet. After shutting the door, she breathes a deep sigh of relief. She turns and leaves the changing area. She enters the waiting room and runs into Jean-Philippe and Anya one last time. They exchange their final goodbyes and Natalie leaves the agency.

Rebecca sits in the living room of her home, watching TV and surfing the internet on her laptop computer. She is doing background research on Jean-Philippe Aristide and likes everything she is finding. He owns agencies in the U.S., France, Argentina, Japan; and each agency stands on its own merits as premier in each region. His name is linked to all the top models across Western Europe and he is known for being the best at molding raw talent. Rebecca is sure that he can make a star out of Natalie. The front door opened, interrupting Rebecca's train of thought. Rebecca stands up and greets her grand-daughter.

"Well," Rebecca asks, "how did it go?"

"It went good." Natalie answers. "He never stopped talking about how great everything was turning out."

"What was your setup" Rebecca asks.

"Very simple." Natalie answers. "He dressed me in white lingerie, gave me the spa treatment, and had me work on a bed covered in pillows. He said it was only going to be an hour, but he wanted to go for another 30 minutes, saying he was getting gold."

"Wonderful!" Rebecca replies. "Natalie, you're a shoe-in for a contract, I can feel it! You just wait. After 24 or 48 hours, we'll be back there, signing on the dotted line, and collecting some fat checks."

"I sure hope so," Natalie says, "my cash flow is down to a trickle."

"Not anymore." Rebecca cuts in. "Follow me upstairs."

The women head upstairs and walk into Rebecca's study. Once inside, Rebecca walks into the closet and opens her safe. She takes out a stack of papers and returns to the desk. Natalie looks at the papers puzzled.

"What's all this?" Natalie asks.

"An investment." Rebecca answers. "An investment in your future, and our continued financial security. Natalie, unbeknownst to your grand-father, early in my life, I was very frugal with my money, and became a smart investor. Every cent I earned went into the stock market. I told Harold, that the pageants were only for trophies and pride, but some of them paid from $5,500 to $10,000. Over time up until now, all my winnings have grown from about $183,000 to $1.72 million."

"NANA!" Natalie shouts, "You're loaded? You're a millionaire!"

"Yes I am," Nana replies, "but don't let it go to your head. I only have this money because I've refused to be wasteful. I've lived in this house for over 40 years, and I've trademarked my name and all my images. This money is funds I don't have to touch, because I'm still getting paid on a daily basis."

"So how does this pertain to me?" Natalie asks.

"Like this." Nana replies. Rebecca hands Natalie sheet of paper resembling a bank statement.

One the statement was Natalie's name, social security number, and an account number. Natalie stared for a moment before noticing the key item on the statement, the monetary amount. $720,000 was transferred into the account for Natalie's own usage.

"NANA!" Natalie exclaimed. "What is this? I can't take… no, I can't take your money!"

"You don't have a choice!" Rebecca responds. "Once you get that contract, you're gonna have to be smart. This is a head start that most girls don't get. This is money you can live off of for a few years before even touching your pay. Use this money as a benchmark. Spend what you need, and invest the rest for your future."

Rebecca takes out a debit card and hands it out to Natalie.

"I'm only going to say this once." Rebecca says. "Take the damn debit card!"

Slowly, Natalie reaches out and takes the card. A tear wells in her eye as she gives her Nana a hug. Rebecca squeezes back and gives her girl a kiss on the cheek. She breaks the embrace when the doorbell rings.

"Shit!" Rebecca exclaims. "That's Etienne. Do me a favor yeah? Answer the door, let him in, and keep him busy for about 20 minutes while I change and get ready. Please?"

"No problem Nana." Natalie answers and heads downstairs.

Natalie arrives downstairs, opens the door and greets Etienne with a big smile.

"Hey Etienne." She says. "Come on in." She steps aside so he can enter.

"Miss Natalie." He says. "It's a pleasure to meet you again."

He takes her right hand and kisses it.

"She's upstairs getting dressed." Natalie continues. "Can I get you anything to drink, coffee, water, vodka?"

"No, thank you." He answers. "I am fine. You spend a lot of time here don't you?"

"Yeah," Natalie answers, "I do, but it's only because she insists that I do."

"It seems like every time I come," he says, "I see you."

"You see me every time you come huh?" She asks. "I'm honored. Does Rebecca know?"

Etienne thinks for a moment then chuckles, catching the innuendo. He playfully shakes a finger at Natalie.

"Dirty mind." He says.

"Dirty girl." She replies.

He enters the living room and takes a seat. Natalie is close behind and sits next to him. He swallows nervously as this is the longest he has ever been around her. He keeps his hands folded in his lap and sits perfectly upright. Natalie catches his apprehension and moves in closer.

"You seem tense." She states. "Big plans tonight?"

"You could say so." He answers. "There is a new restaurant in town. It specializes in down south cuisine. You know, the kind Rebecca was raised on. I'm going to take her there and give her a taste of her native home."

"Aww." Natalie swoons. "That's so sweet! I wish I had a man to do that for me. Is that why you're so nervous?"

"Um…no." He answers. "I want to gauge her reaction and feelings towards me, because I think I might ask her to marry me."

"MARRY YOU?" Natalie shouts.

"Shhhh!" He pleads. "Not so loud. I want it to be a surprise. Besides, I'm just gauging tonight. If all goes well at dinner, I'll come back in a few days and asks her then."

"Ohhh, how romantic!" Natalie says and throws her arms around him.

She squeezes him tight and presses her chest against him. He can smell her sweet scent and becomes aroused. He returns the squeeze and inhales deeply. His arousal becomes visible in his pants. Natalie senses it and presses forward.

"She always said you were the perfect man." She says. "Now I can see why. You're so considerate!"

She withdraws her hug and looks down at his lap. She can see his erection through his pants.

"And hung like a horse!" She exclaims.

He shoots his gaze downwards and quickly crosses his legs, trying to hide his arousal. His movements are so quick, they cause his erection pain.

"I'm so sorry." He grimaces. "That was very rude of me."

"Don't be sorry!" She protests. "Shit, that's something to be proud of. You must've been called the jackhammer in college!"

"Please," he says, "do not discuss this with Rebecca. I don't want her to think I'm a pig or unworthy."

"Hey, hey, it's perfectly normal." She says. "I won't tell. I swear."

With that she quickly reaches into his lap and gives his cock a playful squeeze. He initially jumps, but does not protest the intrusion. His breathing becomes very rapid and his brow is soaked with sweat. Natalie withdraws her hand and places it on his forehead.

"Wow," she says, "you're totally flushed. Let me get you some ice water."

"Yes please." He replies. "Thank you."

Natalie heads to the kitchen to get him a glass of water. Etienne is a very sweet man and she feels he deserves a much better woman than her nana. Plus, she knew it would drive Rebecca mad if he left her for another woman. She would even like a little go round with him herself. With that thought in her mind she hikes up her skirt, shifts the gusset of her panties aside and rubs the rim of the glass against her moist vagina.

Let's give you a little taste of what's out there.

The deed done, she fills the glass with ice and water before returning to the living room. Retaking her seat, she gives him the glass as he thanks her.

He brings the glass to his lips and takes a quick sip. As he pulls the glass away, he breathes deeply, and brings it back to his lips. He drinks the water slowly, but without stopping, and at a steady pace. When the water is finished, he holds the glass in place and continues to inhale deeply.

"Etienne." A voice calls out from the top of the stairs. It was Rebecca.

Quickly, he puts the water down, regains his composure, and stands at attention.

"Yes my love." He answers.

Rebecca saunters down the stairs wearing a black and red evening gown. Her neck is adorned with diamonds, and she smells of his favorite Dior perfume.

"Wow," he stammers, "you look ravishing!"

"Thank you." She replies.

Etienne stands frozen in the living room, just staring at Rebecca. Acting quickly Natalie reaches out and smacks him on the backside, coaxing him into action.

"Don't just stand there." She says. "She's wanting for you."

He reacts to the strike on his ass and walks over to Rebecca. She greets him with a warm smile and a small peck on the lips. He takes her by the hand and leads her to the door. He holds it open so she may pass first, then he steals one last glance at Natalie before he heads out.

Natalie heads back to the couch and reflects on what just happened. Obviously, Etienne was attracted to her, and he is conflicted by this attraction. He wants to stay true to Rebecca and does not want to be deemed "unworthy." She could take advantage of this, and decided to bide her time.

She heads back upstairs to relax. She goes to her bathroom and enjoys a long warm shower. Afterwards, she remains naked, save for her favorite black silk robe, and turns on her television. She surfs the channels and arrives at the Style Channel, the same station from the agency waiting room. Nothing of interest was showing, but she remembered the profile from earlier on the L.A. model, Willow Carter. She turns on her computer, logs on to the internet, and looks her up. Information is a little scarce, but after typing in www.willowcarter.com, she is directed to the website for "Femmes Jolies Modeling Academy."

"Femmes Jolies" is a world-renown modeling agency, and regarded as one of the best agencies west of the Mississippi River. Located in Los Angeles, California, the agency represents over 30 models internationally. The profiles of all the models are listed on the site. Natalie looks up Willow Carter's profile and reads. Her biography reads like the standard Hollywood rocker chick. She has over 30 tattoos, 25 piercings, loves rock and heavy metal, and thinks mean people "suck." The bio also states that she discovered her true self after a traumatic experience in her youth, but does not elaborate on it. She has only been in the industry for 10 months, but has already earned over $120,000 in annual modeling contracts and endorsements. In her personal acknowledgements, she thanks a "Mama Ray," and her "Big Sisters," for allowing her to be who she is and not letting her hold back her larger than life personality.

"Mama Ray?" Natalie mutters to herself.

She does not know why, but the name strikes a chord with her. She cycles through her memory, but cannot recall anyone of significance named Ray. She puts the though in the back of her mind and continues looking through the website. She checks out a few more of the profiles: Stacy Clears, Hera Williams, Jamaica Mungro, Arpi Tahmasian, Greta Van Olfseng, and Isabella De Oro before she gets bored. She clicks back to the agency homepage to find out anything else interesting about it. She clinks on the "Agency History" link and her interest is renewed.

The agency was founded five years ago and through hard work and exhausting hours, enjoys the success it has attained to this day. Natalie reads the name of the founder and her body goes cold: Raylene Cordova.

Raylene Cordova. Raylene Cordova. Raylene Cordova. Raylene Cordova. Raylene Cordova.

The name cycles nonstop through her mind. Over and over and over again, the name repeats, and she can hear it, loud as thunder, blasting against her psyche. She stares hard at the screen, she does not blink, and tears begin to stream down her face and she mutters silent to herself.

"Mom?"

Instantly, her mind flashes back to her memories. She relived every moment her mother yelled at her, and hit her for not living up to her high standards. She remembered and could feel the bruises she received and the ridicule she endured. Each strike cracked like whip and exploded in her mind's eye. She puts her head down and closes her eyes, but the memories do not fade. Instead, they grow stronger and more intense. She feels her skin burn and her blood begins to boil. She pulls at her hair but can not rid herself of the visions. She sees and hears her mother screaming at her, directly in her ear. She can feel her striking her face and leaving a mark, sometimes drawing blood.

She can not stand the visions any longer. She opens her eyes, but the experience worsens. On the screen is a picture of Raylene, in all her radiance. Natalie cries loudly.

"Mom." She cries. "Why mom? Why?"

Those words are all she can say. She had last seen her mother almost seven years ago, but the pain was just as great as ever, and she can not stand it. She closes her laptop and curls in her bed. She lay in a fetal position, unable to move. She is back in her low point and once again feels trapped. Slowly and steadily, she falls asleep and she dreams.

Natalie rises out of bed and looks around. She is not in her bedroom. Instead she is in an empty hotel room. She looks herself over, and notices she is in the white lingerie she wore during the photo shoot. She stands and gets out of the bed. There is a TV on and a woman sitting on the couch watching it. Her back is turned, so Natalie can not see her face, but can clearly see her strawberry blond hair. Natalie slowly walks toward her but stops and looks at the closet. A loud creaking sound is coming from it, and she feels compelled to discover the source. As she gets closer, the sound gets louder. Once she is directly in front of the door, the creaking is unbearably loud. Natalie throws open the door. The creaking stops, but the sight is horrifying.

Inside the closet, a body is hanging by the neck from a noose. The body is female with blonde hair. She is wearing a crimson top, white skirt, and simple Keds, no socks. Her blond hair is covering her face. Blood is running heavily from her left hand.

The left hand!

Natalie looks at her own hand, and sees her scar. The scar from being stuck in a locker while she was physically beaten. She then has a moment of clarity. The crimson top, white skirt, and simple shoes; this was the same outfit she wore on her last day as a victim. Seeing this, Natalie threw back the girl's hair and saw her face, her own face.

Natalie jumps backwards and falls down at the sight. Her lips were busted open and bleeding. Blood rushed from her nose and her left eye was swollen shut. She hung by her neck, and swung lifelessly. Natalie looked at herself in that state and wanted to vomit.

"I thought she was dead!" A woman's voice rings out.

Natalie snaps her vision to the woman on the couch. The woman's head began to move, but her face is still not visible. She picks up a glass of wine and takes a sip.

"Guess I was wrong." She says.

"Who are you?" Natalie asks.

"That doesn't matter." The woman answers. "The question is; who are you?"

"What?" Natalie asks. "I don't understand."

"That's the problem." The woman responds. "You never did!"

With that statement, the woman snaps her fingers and the room flashes white. Natalie puts her hand up to shield her eyes from the blinding light. The flash only lasts for a split second. When it fades, Natalie looks around. Her surroundings have not changed and she is still on the floor, but her left hand is cut and hurts like hell, she can barely see out of her left eye, her mouth is bleeding and her stomach is in burning pain. She hunches over to control the pain, but it is almost intolerable.

"Oh, fuck!" Natalie yells and the pain overpowers her.

When Natalie looks herself over, she is now wearing the crimson top, white skirt, and simple shoes. She looks at the closet, and sees that it is empty.

"Same ol' Natalie." The woman says.

"WHO THE FUCK ARE YOU?" Natalie screams.

"Don't take that tone with me young lady." The woman shoots back.

She raises the TV remote and turns the set off. She stands up off the couch and walks around to the back, towards Natalie. When she is on the other side, Natalie can finally see her face.

"Mom?" Natalie asks.

"I've always hated when you called me that." Raylene says.

Natalie tries to speak, but the words will not come out.

"Getting rid of you," Raylene continues, "was the best decision I ever made. You were hopeless back then, and you still are now. Giving birth to you was the biggest mistake of my life."

The words stab Natalie like a dull knife through the heart. Raylene walks closer to Natalie, squats down, and leans in face to face.

"You know," she goes on, "if I wasn't so desperate for a contract with that agency 20 years ago, you never would have been born, and I would have been happy. Instead, I had to put my life on hold for 12 years, dragging your ass behind me, like a lazy dog that doesn't want to walk."

Natalie's tears run in streams down her face. She wants to stop her mother, lash out in some kind of way, but she is unable to. She is helpless and cannot move. Raylene turns her head slightly, and then quickly looks back at Natalie and slaps her hard across the face.

"Why are you crying?!" she demands. "You stop that this instant! When the fuck are you going to grow up, and stop being a whiny little brat?"

Natalie cannot answer. She can only increase the intensity of her cries. Without warning, Raylene grabs Natalie by her throat and squeezes tightly, cutting off her air. Natalie struggles to breathe, but can not force her mother off.

"Some things never change!" Raylene states. "I have all the control, and you are still worthless!"

Natalie's vision blurs as she loses oxygen. Her body shakes, she goes cold, and everything goes black.

Gasping for air, Natalie shoots up from her bed in a cold sweat. She rubs her throat, coughs loudly, and sucks in the sweet cold air that fills her lungs. Holding her neck, she looks around, and sees that she is back in her room. Her television is on, her laptop is on the floor, and her lights are on. The only difference is that it is daylight coming through her window. It was morning, and Natalie realizes that she slept through the night, trapped in the grip of that nightmare. She tries to relax her breathing and calm down, but is not given a chance as her door burst open and Rebecca storms in.

"What the fuck did you do yesterday?" Rebecca demands.

"Wha…what?" Natalie stammers.

"Don't play stupid with me young lady." Rebecca replies. "What happened at the shoot yesterday? The one with Jean-Philippe."

Natalie thinks for a moment, then remembers the shoot.

"It went well." She replies. "He said I was great and said I should be signed any day now."

"What did he same exactly?" Nana asks.

"He said I was beautiful." Natalie answers. "He said I was a vision and he lo-"

"A vision?" Rebecca cuts her off. "He called you a vision? Oh fuck! Why didn't you tell me this?"

"He complimented me!" Natalie protests. "What's wro-"

"Compliment?" Again Rebecca cuts her off. "You thought he was complimenting you? Shit Natalie, a vision is not good! A vision means he's seen it before, and doesn't care to see it again."

Natalie reflects back to her quick chat with the model named Lynn at the agency.

"Haven't I taught you any thing?" Rebecca asks. "Why didn't protest? You should have protested! You should have demanded to know what exactly you did wrong. You should have made amends. Now, you're screwed. He'll never sign you now!"

"There will be other agencies!" Natalie interjected.

"We don't want other agencies!" Rebecca roars. "We want this one! I just got off the phone with the happy little faggot, and he has no intention of signing you. He tries to by polite, and sweet, and sugary about it, saying he's not sure of your look, but that's just bullshit! The truth is that you're nothing more than dog shit to him. How could you not fucking see that?"

"We'll be alright Nana!" Natalie insists. "Let's me go back, and see..."

"Shut up!" Rebecca demands. "Just shut up Natalie. No way you're going back there to talk to him. You've done enough damage already. I have to fix this mess. I'm going there right now. I'll probably be gone all day. Don't you dare go anywhere! You stay here and fix whatever the fuck is wrong with you." She storms out of the room.

Natalie is stunned. The other model was right, Jean-Philippe told her straight up that she had no chance, and all Natalie did was smile at him. She slowly sits on the bed and hangs her head. She feels like such a disappointment.

Not your fault!

Natalie shots her head up. That voice, she had heard it before. It had been silent for six months, but it returns to her. High, meek and a quiet whisper, yet very assertive.

Set up to fail!

"No." Natalie asserts. "I can't fail! I've come too far."

She stands in your way!

"No she doesn't." Natalie responds. "She wants to live off my success. I can't succeed if she makes me fail. She's greedy like that."

Jealous!

"Yes." She agrees, "Very jealous. Life is passing her by, and she can't keep up."

Different avenue!

"Different avenue?" Natalie asks.

Now she is confused. She did not understand the meaning of a different avenue. As if on queue, her laptop beeps. Natalie looks down and sees that it is unplugged. She never shut it down and the battery was running low in hibernation mode. She picks it up, opens it to properly shut it down, and freezes. On the screen is a picture of her mother. The laptop was still on the webpage for her agency. The phrase now clicks in her mind.

"She'd never sign me!" Natalie protests.

She's forgotten about you!

The possibility stabs her in the heart.

"It's been so long." She stammers.

She never loved you.

Tears begin to run down her face.

"I know." She acknowledges.

Neither has Nana!

Natalie's sadness turns to anger.

"I know." She replies.

The acknowledgement turns her anger to rage.

They've despised you!

"I know." She cries.

Her rage turns to hate.

You know what you must do!

She lets her hate consume her.

"Absolutely." She affirms.

Jean-Philippe Aristide arrives to his studio and kisses the models on the set. He takes his seat and begins directing the shoot in his heavy French accent. He is pleased with the actions of his models and is showering them with praise. After 15 minutes pass, an intern comes onto the set and whispers in his ear.

"Merde!" He mutters under his breath. "Pardon, pardon, I am so sorry. I have to attend to zee, how you say, unexpected business. Anya my dear, give zem five, and zen continue vith zee vinter motif. Merci, mon amoure."

He leaves the set. Arriving at the waiting room, he puts on his best possible smile and greets his visitor.

"Rebecca." He exclaims. "Comment t'allez vous?"

He hugs her and kisses her cheeks. She returns the greeting in kind.

"Je vais mal." She replies. "Tres mal!"

"Oh, no my dear." He responds. "Vhat is zee matter?"

"Not here." She answers. "Can we go to a private room?"

"Mais oui!" He replies.

He turns to the intern at the front desk.

"Jasmine," he says, "pas de telephone s'il vous plait."

He puts his arm around Rebecca's shoulders and leads her to a conference room in the back of the building. After locking the door, he turns to address her.

"Merci," he begins, "I appreciate zee need you have for zee discretion."

"Let's just say I'm doing you a favor." She rips back. "Tell me right now Jean-Philippe, and don't sugarcoat it. What's wrong with Natalie? Why won't you sign her?"

"My dear," he says, "don't get me wrong. Votre grande fille, she truly a beautiful girl, a fine specimen she is, but she does not fit zee need I have for zee moment."

"What the hell does that mean?" She asks. "What need could she not fill? You've seen her, those striking eyes, those long firm leg, those bouncy tits. What more do you want?"

"Ses caractéristiques sont très jolies!" He exclaims. "Zey are not zee problem. Zee issue is zee character. Her aura."

"What's wrong with her aura?" She asks.

"She is a soft and delicate flower." He answers. "She is a beautiful girl, oui, but she is also safe. Zere is no mystery, no danger, and no risks. She needs zee hint of enigma, because right now, vat you see in her, is vat you get."

"I sent you her pictures beforehand." Rebecca interjects. "You're telling me that you could not see that before you agreed to screen her?"

"No," he answers, "I could not see it. Zee photos you sent me vere taken by Clay Sautier. New York and London may love him, but his work is not fit to vipe zee shit from my ass. But I saw zee potential in your girl."

"And all her potential is strictly in softness?" She asks.

"Oui." He answers. "Zis is not zee bad zing. I can always use a soft girl for a good amount a vork, but you must understand, I am flooded vith zee soft girls, and on zee day of her shoot, I lost my best danger girl."

"What does that have to do with Natalie?" She asks.

"I have to make zee money." He responds. "At zee ends of zee day, I find my girl, Lynn Harper, unconscious and beaten in a broom closet. I need a replacement vhile she is on zee mend. I vanted Natalie, but my cameras do not lie and I cannot take her. I am so sorry."

He heads to the door to exit. She scoots over and blocks his path.

"Sit down." She asserts.

"Mademoiselle," he begins, "zere is nothing else…"

"I said sit down." She says slightly louder and points to a chair.

"I have a deadline to…" he starts but is cuts off angrily.

"SIT YOUR SWEET ASS DOWN YOU FUCKING FAGGOT!" She yells.

He drops into the seat. Rebecca calmly straightens her hair and sits next to him.

"I don't know," she begins, "what it's going to take, but I will hold you here against your will, all night if I have to, until I convince you to take a second look at Natalie."

He lowers his head in quiet resignation.

"J'ecoute." He says.

"Merci." She replies.

Etienne pulls into the driveway of Rebecca's house. The date the previous night went well, and he feels comfortable to ask for her hand. He was surprised to receive an email from her, about two hours ago at 2:15pm to meet her at the house between 4:00pm and 5:00pm. He never liked keeping his love waiting so he got there as soon as he could. He gets out of his car and walks up the porch steps. He is about to ring the doorbell, when he notices the door is open slightly. He rings the bell anyway, but when there is not answer, he sticks his head in and calls out.

"Becca!" He calls. No response.

He steps into the entry and shuts the door. He calls her name again still with no response. He hears slightly muffled cries coming from upstairs. He calls out but still gets no response. He runs upstairs, fearing the worse. He gets upstairs, and the cries get louder and more distinct. The more he hears them, he realizes, those are not cries. Those are moans, and they are coming from one of the bedrooms, not Rebecca's. Wanting to be sure and now with a measure of curiosity, he opens a bedroom. He stares in silent amazement.

On the bed he sees Natalie. Her black robe is sprawled open and she is completely naked underneath. Her breasts are out, her legs are spread apart, and she is masturbating while watching pornography on her laptop. She is not disturbed as he enters the room, and doesn't seem to notice. Her eyes are closed and her head is thrown back in splendid ecstasy. She moans softly as her left hand rubs her breasts and her right hand works her cunt. Her moans get progressively louder as she appears to approach orgasm.

She opens her eyes slightly and turns her head towards Etienne, but she doesn't stop. Her eyes grow a little wider and they lock with his. He knows he should leave her alone, but instead he ventures further into the room, standing next to her bed side. He sweats profusely as he watches her masturbate. She raises her right hand from her gash and places on the front of his pants, squeezing his hardening penis. He moans at her touch and does not resist. Using the same hand, she unbuckles his belt, unbuttons and unzips his trousers, and fishes his dick from his underwear. Slowly and gently, she strokes it along the entire length, keeping a steady rhythm. He closes his eyes and places his hand on hers. Against his better judgment, he now belonged to her.

Taking the next step, Natalie leans forward and takes his penis into her mouth. She sucks gently on the head before moving forward down the length of the shaft. She gets a steady back and forth rhythm while using her hand to massage his balls.

Etienne is delirious. His head is spinning and a warm, relaxing sensation engulfs his entire body. The pleasure is not without guilt. He wants her to stop. He knows he is wrong and should push her away. He reaches out with his hand to stop her, but instead places it on the back of her head, encouraging her actions. He can feel the pressure building. The friction and smoothness of her mouth is driving him over the edge, and he cannot stop. He tenses up, lets out a loud gasp, and stops pumping. Natalie holds her position and keeps his organ in her mouth. He explodes in climax, sending his seed flying down her throat, spilling out the corners of her mouth. She holds her suction firm and does not relent.

When his orgasm passes, she looks up at him seductively and resumes her task, taking him down her throat. In a fit of passion, he rips off his shirt, grabs her leg, and spins her around so her legs are over the edge of the bed. He drops to his knees and dives in, feasting hungrily on her treats.

Natalie enjoys the sensations she is feeling. Her eyes are closed, her head is thrown back, and she rides the wave of pleasure. He sucks eagerly on her clit, licking and drinking the excreted juices. He uses his fingers and she shouts her approval. He uses his tongue effectively and brings her to multiple orgasms. When his erection returns, he stands up and buries it to the hilt inside of her. He thrusts like a man possessed, grabbing her hips and driving into her at full bore. He cannot last very long, as hers is the tightest vagina he has ever experienced. Within a few minutes, he withdraws his phallus and spills his semen all over her abdomen and chest.

Exhausted, he collapses on the bed next to her breathing hard. He rolls onto his back and continues to pant. Natalie is tired as well, but she moves slowly towards his waist and returns his penis to her mouth, sucking at gently. He grunts in initial pain, as he is very sensitive at this point. His energy returns quickly, but his shame takes control of him. He begins to sob over his actions, and removes Natalie from her fellatio. He jumps off the bed and puts his pants back on.

"I am a dog!" He cries. "I have failed her! I'm not worth her love!"

He picks his shirt up off the floor, throws it on quickly and flees the bedroom. Natalie does not plea or try to stop him. Instead, she rolls onto her back, smiles, and continues to masturbate. She is pleased with herself. Her job was done, and it was fun to do.

Rebecca is mentally drained. She spent almost the entire day trying to negotiate a second screening for Natalie. Jena-Philippe was very resistant and incredibly stubborn, but eventually, he yielded and scheduled another shoot for Natalie to occur the following week. Rebecca had never had to fight so hard for something in her life, but is glad to have accomplished her goal. She exits the freeway and guns down her street in a hurry. She wants to get home, inform Natalie of what happened, take a warm bath, and maybe summon Etienne over to help 'relax her.'

As she approaches her home, she is pleasantly surprised to see Etienne's car parked in the driveway. He must have come over to surprise her. She would enjoy his company and looks forward to thanking him properly. She parks on the street and exits.

She walks up the walkway to the porch, and is surprised to see Etienne run out. His face is red and he looks like he is distraught. She grows concerned and runs to comfort him.

"Etienne," she begins, "oh my God, what's wrong?"

She grabs his arm lovingly. He violently shakes her grasp.

"DON'T TOUCH ME!" He yells. "I have failed you!"

He rushes to his car, and she is close behind. She grabs him again more forcefully.

"What do you mean failed me?" she demands.

"I'm a dog." He says. "Unworthy of your love."

"Let me decided that." She interjects. "Just calm down."

"No." He responds. "I have not been true to you. I have strayed."

"What?" She asks in disbelief. "How? When? With who?"

"It doesn't matter." He cries. "I can be with you no longer."

"What!" She shouts. "You're leaving me.?"

"It is best." He says as he climbs into his car and starts the engine.

"No, wait!" She protests in tears. "We can get through this."

He reaches out and gently touches her face. He is truly in love with her. She touches his hand, enjoying the warmth of his touch. She desperately wants him to stay, but he resists her.

"I'm sorry." He says. "I will always hold you special my love."

He zips out of the driveway and takes off down the street, leaving Rebecca's life forever. She calls out after him in one last desperate cry, but he disappears out of sight. She falls to her knees and cries loudly. She looses her self-control and screams for the love she has just lost.

Natalie got out of bed when she heard her Nana arrive, and witnessed the whole scene. She smiles and congratulates herself on a job well done. She goes to her laptop, opens her Nana's email sent box, and deletes the email she sent to Etienne earlier that day. She then takes a shower.

Out of her shower, Natalie puts her robe back on and walks outside the bathroom. She can hear her Nana crying. She slowly tip-toes to the door and listens for a few minutes. Natalie's conscience takes over, and she feels she should say something to make her feel better. She leans lightly onto the door, and whispers very softly.

"Cry bitch, cry" She whispers. "Cry me a fucking river."

Natalie feels much better now. She returns to her room and retires for the night.

At 9:23am, Saturday, the following morning, Rebecca bursts into Natalie's room, waking the girl up. She heads to her closet. She starts grabbing handfuls of clothes and throwing them on the floor.

"Change this shit!" She demands. "All of it!"

"Nana," Natalie says, "what are you doing?"

Rebecca steps up to Natalie, grabs her by the hair and yanks her to the closet.

"Oww!" Natalie yells. "What the fuck?"

"You see all this shit?" Nana yells. "All this cutesy, sexy, feminine, girlish shit? This is why he won't sign you! You're too fucking safe! You're soft and elegant. You have no danger, or sense of danger or mystery. You're too fucking good!"

She lets go of Natalie's hair and the girl falls on the floor.

"I had to argue my ass off to get you second chance." Nana says. "Change your look! Get some danger in you!"

She picks up a pile of clothes and throws them on Natalie.

"I have to go somewhere this morning." She continues. "I'll be back late tonight. You have until then to show me how much you appreciate all I have done for you, or else your ass is back in the basement. Do you understand?"

She does not wait for an answer. Instead she turns around and heads for the door.

"Nana." Natalie calls out.

Rebecca turns around and faces her grand-daughter.

"You have no idea," she continues, "how dangerous I can be."

She stares hard at her Nana, her mind made up. Rebecca turns around and exits the room.

Natalie rolls onto her back, laying face up next to a pile of clothes. She knows what she must do; she just wants to know how.

Dig!

A thought flashes through her mind and she thinks hard about it.

Dig!

The same thought, only accompanied by the voice, that sinister, meek voice.

Dig!

She gets off the floor, throws some clothes on, and heads downstairs to the backyard.

Hours pass…

Rebecca returns from her day out. She returned to the agency to work out the details of the shoot with Jean-Philippe that morning. When she was done, she went to see Etienne, and attempted to restore their relationship, to no avail. Exhausted and distraught, she returned home. She wants to check on Natalie's progress, and retire afterwards.

She pulls into the driveway and cuts the engine. She gets out of the car and shuts the door. The time is 10:46pm, and she can barely see three feet in front of her face. She looks around and sees the outline of her home in the moonlight. The porch is very difficult to see because the porch light is not turned on.

Cursing under her breath, she slowly heads to the front door, tripping over the first few steps of the porch. Reaching the front door, she unlocks the deadbolt and enters her home. No lights are inside, so only the moonlight illuminates the foyer. She reaches over to the nearby wall and flips the light switch.

Nothing happens.

"What the hell?" She mutters to herself.

She tries a few more times with the same result. The power was out. She takes smalls steps in the direction of the kitchen, but slips on a sheet of paper. She lands hard on her backside and elbows.

"FUCK!" She yells. "NATALIE?"

Her calls go unanswered. She calls for her grand daughter again, but is only greeted with silence. She reaches inside her purse and withdraws her lighter. After a few flicks, the flame ignites, giving her a small amount of light. She picks up the paper she slipped on earlier and looks at it, intrigued. It was a printout from the website of the local newspaper, dated roughly six months ago.

DEATH AND BRUTALITY AT WSU!

Another student was found brutally murdered on the WSU campus. This second, possibly third, murder dumbfounds investigators, and sparks panic amongst the alumni and students.

Rebecca read the beginning of the article. The student's name was Howard Haynesworth, and he was brutally hacked to death. She puts the paper down, disgusted and appalled. She hoists her lighter, gets to her feet and freezes. Another article is tacked to the wall.

STUDENT SUFFERS FATAL REACTION AT FRAT PARTY!

Rebecca remembers reading this article. The young woman was the first of six students to die that year on campus. Rebecca takes the article down and ponders for a moment.

"Why would Natalie print these out?" She asks herself.

She calls for Natalie again, but no one responds. She walks further into the house, and finds more articles. She reads each headline.

STUDENT FOUND DEAD IN COLLEGE POOL.

BLACK YOUTH FOUND RAPED AND RUN DOWN ON BACK COUNTRY ROAD.

MISSING STUDENT FEARED DEAD BY POLICE.

BODY OF MISSING STUDENT FOUND.

DEADLY REACTION MAY HAVE BEEN SABATOGE!

ANOTHER STUDENT FOUND DEAD, BURIED AT CONSTRUCTION SITE.

DEADLY YEAR AT WESTIN STATE FINALY ENDS!

Rebecca is confused. She does not understand why Natalie would want to relive those horrible moments from college. She reaches the kitchen and turns off her lighter. The moonlight penetrates brightly into the kitchen and she can see rather clearly. She looks out into the backyard and her confusion grows. She sees a large mound of dirt next to a large hole, with more dirt flying out. Is someone digging in her yard? She peers harder and sees a flash of blond hair. She races out the back door. Once in the backyard she hurries toward the hole.

"NATALIE!" She calls out. "What the fuck are you doing?"

Rebecca arrives at the hole, but the girl does not respond.

"Put the damn shovel down and answer me!" She shouts.

Natalie complies. She stops digging, throws the shovel on the ground by Nana's feet and climbs out of the hole. Once out, she picks up the shovel, but remains silent.

"Where the fuck do I begin?" Nana asks. "The power going out, the house is a mess, the articles all over the house, you digging this big ass hole. What is wrong with you?

"Nothing." Natalie answers.

"Don't give me that shit!" Rebecca replies angrily. "Are you fucked in the head?"

"Oh Nana," Natalie responds, "I've never had more clarity than I have now."

"Clarity?" Rebecca shouts "You call this clarity? Why doesn't anything work in the house?"

"I cut the power." Natalie answers sharply.

"Why the hell would you cut the power?" Rebecca demands. Natalie doesn't answer, only smiles at her.

"Bitch," Rebecca replies, "you better make sure your head is on right, because I'm just about ready to throw you out. Why did you cut the power, and why are those articles all over my house?"

"HA!" Natalie blurts. "You noticed? Good!"

She turns her back to her Nana and takes a few steps away.

"Don't turn your back on me young lady." Rebecca says, her temper rising. "Now you answer me. Why are those articles all over my house?"

"By themselves," Natalie answers, "yes, they are just articles. Lonely little articles, with no purpose other than to report the goings on of the world around you; a world you don't give two shits about."

Rebecca takes a small step forward, more confused than ever.

"Separately," Natalie continues, "they are meaningless. But together, they represent so much more. Something wonderful, something magnificent, and something much more than just a report."

"Wonderful and magnificent?" Rebecca asks. "My mind is spinning. What the fuck is so magnificent and wonderful about students getting killed?"

"Because," Natalie continues, "together, they are not reports. Together, they are my confession."

"Your Confess-"

CRACK!

Natalie moves quickly. She swings on her pivot foot, raises the shovel, and spins around to face her Nana, swinging the shovel at full force. The blade of the shovel strikes Rebecca bluntly on the nose, knocking her back, reeling to the ground.

The force of the strike sends Rebecca flying to the ground. She lands hard on her back in the dirt. She is dizzy and woozy, but still conscious. Her vision is blurred, she cannot breathe out of her shattered nose, her hearing is muffled, and she can feel her warm blood pour over her face. As she ponders her situation and panics, she is struck again, this time across the chest, knocking the wind out of her.

Natalie rears the shovel backs and strikes her Nana repeatedly. With each strike, Rebecca's body is bruised and her bones are broken.

"I confess," Natalie begins between strikes, "to doing what I had to do." (Strike) "I confess," (Strike), "to killing those," (Strike) "that sought to torture me" (Strike) "I confess," (Strike), "to hating you," (Strike), "with every inch," (Strike), "of," (Strike), "my," (Strike), "being!" (Strike)

Natalie stops striking and leans on the shovel for support. Her breathing is heavy as she pants. Rebecca is sprawled on the ground. Her face is covered in the blood she coughs up, her breathing is very shallow, and her eyes begin to roll up in her head. Natalie stands straight and places the blade of the shovel against her Nana's throat.

"You're just like them Nana." She says. "So now it's time to join them!"

Rebecca tries to protest and plea for her life, but she cannot. Natalie jumps on the shovel and presses all the weight on the blade. It slices through Rebecca's throat, spilling her blood all over the dirt, and decapitating her head from her body. Natalie raises the shovel and swings it like a hockey stick, batting Nana's head into the open hole. She then bends down, grabs the carcass by the arm, and drags it into the hole.

Returning to the pile of dirt, she begins to refill the hole. Hours fly by while she shovels, and by the early hours of the morning, she is finished. She is exhausted after her tireless night of work, and she has to pee. As a final insult to injury, she drops her pants, squats down, and pisses on her Nana's grave. Afterwards, she walks inside the house.

Natalie climbs the stairs, goes to her bathroom, and strips naked. She studies herself in the mirror. Her arms, hands, and face are covered in dirt and Nana's blood. Her hair is caked with mud, and her body is red with exhaustion, but she does not feel fatigued. She turns on the hot water and jumps in the shower.

In the shower, she feels the dirt and blood melt from her body. She feels no sadness or remorse over what she just did, only a sense of accomplishment and uplifting. That feeling is followed by a feeling of emptiness.

What now?

She does not know what is next. All she knows, is that there is nothing left for her here. Nana was the last bastion of her childhood, but she still feels the weight upon her shoulders.

Why won't it go away?

She closes her eyes and tries to focus, but her mind is jumbled. She reopens her eyes and looks down. Glancing at her shoulders, she freezes. She stares at her blond hair and freezes. She closes her eyes and sees an image flash. It passes quickly, but begins to give her clarity.

Mom?

Natalie has the same blond locks as her mother. Her mind flashes the image again, and her mother cycles through her thoughts.

New life. New beginning.

Natalie makes her decision. There is nothing left for her in Oregon. She wants to leave her past life behind, but to remain in the house of painful memories would not help. She exits the shower, dries off, and heads to her bedroom.

Once in her room, she turns on her computer and signs on to a travel website. She buys a same day one-way ticket to Los Angeles using the debit card her Nana gave her a few days earlier. She pays $245 for the ticket. She grabs her luggage and packs all of her essential items like clothes, toiletries, and other items. Still not feeling fatigued, she uses UBER to pick her up and take her to the airport. She takes one last look at the house as the cab pulls away, determined to never return there again.

Seven forty-five in the morning and an alarm clock sounds, sending a loud audible beeping through the bedroom. Raylene Cordova hits the off button and sits up in her warm king size bed. She puts her arms over her head and stretches, her body waking from her deep slumber. She turns her head to the right, stares out the window, and her eyes welcome the Sunday morning glow.

Her bedroom is huge, 30ft by 30ft, equaling 900 square feet. French doors adorned the south wall, leading to a patio overlooking the breath taking Hollywood Hills. Her bed rests on her west wall, and is dressed in silk sheets and a down comforter; lots of pillows. The walls are all white and match the vibrancy of the white furniture. On the wall opposite the bed holds a 65" plasma television with a full surround sound setup. The sunlight permeates through the windows and lights the room in its gentle glow. Raylene has worked hard for this bedroom, and it brings a smile to her face every morning.

She tries to quietly slink out of bed, but she feels a hand reach up and grab her shoulder. She starts to giggle before she is yanked back to the mattress. Two large arms wrap around her upper body and waist, and fingers begin to tickle her. She laughs hysterically while unable to control her body contortions. The fingers finally relent, allowing her to turn and face her attacker.

"Michael!" she shouts and smacks him on the chest. "You handsome jerk!"

"Good morning to you too, sexy!" He responds.

Michael Milton is an Academy Award winning producer, and Raylene's fiancée. He met Raylene during the infancy of his career and was smitten by the darling woman, 12 years his junior. He courted her during an audition for a part in his first feature film, a role she did not get. They kept in contact afterwards. While he tried to get her discovered, she tried to start a modeling agency. She found a few girls willing to sign with her, but with few contacts, she was not a desired location for local models. One fateful day, she brought the few models she could sign to his production studio. The girls fit a casting need he desperately needed to fill, and they all were cast in the film. The movie was a summer blockbuster, and all the girls launched successful acting careers. They continued to model for Raylene, bring her lucrative business and a financial windfall. After a year, Raylene's agency became the target destination for aspiring young models from across the country. Michael continued to use her models for roles in his movies, and they fell in love. Within three years, they were engaged, and more.

"How'd you sleep?" She asks.

"Fantastic." He replies. "But I'm still a little worn out."

"Oh." She says. "I guess we'll just have to work on your stamina."

She climbs on top of him and they begin to kiss deeply. She straddles his waist and begins to grind his stiffening penis. Morning sex is a normal routine for them, and this morning will be no exception, they hope.

"EWWWW!" A voice screeches. "That's so gross!"

Raylene quickly rolls off her man, covers herself with the covers and looks at the little spectator.

"Domi!" She yelps. "Don't you knock?"

'Domi' is short for Dominique, as in Dominique Marie Cordova; Raylene and Michael's five year old daughter. Eighteen months after Raylene arrived in Los Angeles, she and Michael became intimate and she became pregnant. While initially fearful,

Michael quickly comforted her and she decided to move in with him. After Domi was born, Raylene and Michael decided to live together and raise the family. When Domi turned four, Raylene's agency was so successful, she was able to single-handedly purchase an extravagant home in the Hollywood Hills, where the family lives to this day. Domi has the same blonde locks as her mother, and bright green eyes. She is a very loving child, and is quick to embrace and kiss anyone she sees as a family friend. Domi runs into the bedroom and swan dives onto the bed. She is scooped up and held by her father who commences a full bore tickle assault. She squeals with delight.

"Give me the little rascal." Raylene jokes and rescues her daughter.

Domi embraces her mother and snuggles close.

"How's my pretty, pretty girl this morning?" Raylene asks.

"Fine mommy." Domi answers. "Yesterday, at school, Teddy said he would give me a dollar if I did a cartwheel in my dress."

"What?" Raylene asks shocked. "I hope you didn't do it."

"I didn't." Domi replies. "I told him that I'm a lady, and ladies don't do stupid things for money."

"That's my girl." Raylene responds. "Mommy's smart little princess."

"Yes I am!" Domi replies jokingly. "I told him to come back with ten dollars, then I might."

"Why you little!" Raylene roars.

She pounces on the little girl and tickles her mercilessly. Michael reaches over and joins in the fun. They tickle her until she turns purple before they relent. Then they lay in bed as a family and watch Domi's favorite morning cartoons.

At 3:48pm in the afternoon, a flight from Portland, Oregon arrives at the Los Angeles airport. The plane parks and the passengers file out into the terminal. As Natalie exits the plane, she takes a second to close her eyes, and breathe in her first gulp of L.A. air. She can taste the difference from home and embraces it. The air is dirty, think, choking, and venomous, just like her. After securing her luggage from the baggage claim, she heads outside to hail a cab. Out in the open, the hustle and bustle of the second largest city in the country strikes her like a ton of bricks. Cars are lined bumper to bumper and the roadway resembles a parking lot. Horns blare loudly and drivers yell profanities out their windows. As the traffic light turns green, the current stack of cars drive away, and a new bunch fills the vacant space. Once the light is red again, the previous scene repeats itself.

She takes a second to people-watch, and get a feel for the locals. At first, she only encounters folks from out of town, seeking a little adventure in the City of Angels. She hears a young woman saying she is glad to be home and watches her for a second. She is on a cell phone, talking loudly to a caller on the other end. She keeps looking at her fingernails, blowing bubbles with her chewing gum, and every other word out of her mouth is 'like.' She is wearing tight blue jeans, black boots, and a pink halter top with a matching Stetson. She walks away while still yakking it up and swaying her hips from left to right.

Natalie walks to the curb and a blue and white cab pulls up to her. The driver gets out and places her bags in the trunk. He holds the door for her to enter, and closes it behind her. After he climbs in the driver seat, he resets his meter.

"Hello Miss." He says in a Latin accent. "Welcome to Los Angeles."

"Thank you." She replies. "Glad I could be here."

"Where to?" He asks.

"I don't know." She answers. "This was kind of a spur of the moment type of thing. My God, I don't even have a place to stay."

"Hotels are everywhere," He replies, "and they always have vacancies."

"Which one would you recommend?" She asks, "A nice motel that doesn't cost too much."

"There is a Hilton," He answers, "over on Sepulveda Blvd. Very nice, and not too much money."

"Sounds good." She replies. "Take me there."

"No problem Miss." He responds.

The driver heads for the motel, all the while making idle chatter about the current events around the city. She learns about the latest celebrity gossip and he takes her on a quick tour of the Bel-Air neighborhood of Beverly Hills. She asks about the Femmes-Jolies Modeling Agency. He does not have much information about it, but he has heard of it and tells her that it is located in Century City, about 20 minutes away from her hotel. When they reach the Hilton, he unloads her bags and thanks her for her patronage. She pays the faire and tips very handsomely.

At the door to the hotel, a bellboy takes her bags and offers to hold them for her. She makes her way to the front desk and waits for a clerk. A woman looking to be in her early thirties assists her.

"Good afternoon." She says in perky, southern tone with a big smile. "Welcome to the Hilton on Sepulveda, where we guarantee you a pleasurable and relaxing hotel experience. May I have the name of the reservation?"

"No name." Natalie answers. "I just came to town on a whim. I was hoping you had a vacancy."

"Alrighty." The clerk says, keeping her chipper demeanor. "Let me see what I have available for you my dear."

She types feverishly on her computer for a minute before finding some information.

"Okay." She continues. "I have a business suite available. It's on the 13th floor, has a patio, a queen size bed and a view of the L.A. Basin."

"That sounds great!" Natalie quips. "How much per night?"

"Without a reservation," the clerk answers, "we would have to charge you the rush rate of $119 a night. I hope that's not too much."

"No, no," Natalie replies, "that sounds great. I'll take it."

"Great," the clerk responds, "glad you can stay with us. I'll just need some information to make this reservation. You name please?"

"Natalie Renee Cordova." Natalie answers.

"Cordova, Natalie R." The clerk says to herself. "And the length of your stay?"

Natalie never considered how long she would be in town.

"Um…I don't know." Natalie answers. "I didn't think about that. Do I have to give you a certain date?"

"Well, we prefer one." The clerk says. "How about this? I'll put you down for two weeks, and I'll set up a reservation for you immediately following. That way, you can officially check-out, but if you're not ready to leave, we'll just check you back into the room; at the lower rate."

The clerk gives Natalie a playful wink. Natalie responds with a modest chuckle.

"Thank you." Natalie says. "I'd really appreciate that."

"Wonderful." The clerk replies. "I just need a major credit card and an I.D, and we can finalize this process."

Natalie gives the clerk her debit card and her driver's license. The two ladies make friendly chatter while conducting the transaction. Natalie tells her about her hometown in Oregon and the clerk let's her know about the many sights and sounds of Los Angeles.

"Okay, it appears we are all set." The clerk says and gives the items back to Natalie. "Is there anything else at all I can do for you?"

"Yes," Natalie answers, "two things. First, I like you. What's your name?"

"Oh." The clerk squeals and pats her chest. "Looks like I forgot to where my name badge."

She extends her hand to Natalie.

"I'm Valerie." She says. "Valerie Davis, originally from Tuscaloosa, Alabama."

"All the way from Alabama?" Natalie asks.

"Born and raised." Valerie answers. "Roll Tide!"

Natalie chuckles, catching the college reference.

"Second," Natalie says, "do you have any information on the Femme-Jolies Modeling Agency?"

"So you're an aspiring model huh?" Valerie asks back.

"I dunno," Natalie answers, "but I do love the business. I figure I might as well do some star searching while I'm here."

Valerie reaches under her desk and pulls out a brochure.

"This is the info we have on them." She says. "The phone numbers and address is on the back. I heard that a lot of movie stars like to travel there and recruit new talents. Maybe you'll be discovered."

Her computer beeps and Valerie withdraws a keycard.

"Ok my dear," She says, "here is your key and your room is 1331."

"Thank you so much Valerie." Natalie says.

"You're welcome." Valerie replies. "The elevators are over there to your right. Go on up to your room and just call the desk when you're ready for your bags."

"Alright." Natalie says. "Thanks again."

Natalie takes her keycard and heads for the elevators. In the elevator hall, she encounters another L.A. local. Like the woman at the airport, he is also on a cell phone, but he is professionally dressed in a taupe three-button suit. Natalie can't understand the context of his conversation, but he speaks very clearly and appears to be finalizing a contract of some sort. He steals a glance at Natalie and leaves the hall, as though he cannot allow anyone to hear him speak.

The elevator arrives and Natalie enters. She presses the 13th floor button and makes her accent. Arriving at her destination, she easily finds her room. It is of decent size, standard faire for a hotel room, with a private bathroom and easy access to the balcony. Instead of taking her time to look around, Natalie picks up the phone and begins to dial.

It's late in the afternoon and Keri Hardigan, a recent college grad and intern, is finalizing a financial report for the Femmes-Jolies Modeling Agency. The past quarter has bees an overwhelming success and she was sure her boss would be pleased at the report. She takes one last look at her operating statement and is very happy with the results. The Agency has earned $2 million worth of annual contracts for the final month of the quarter and $7.52 million over the whole quarter. Very little money was spent on overhead and payrolls were kept low, with minimal overtime. As she scans the results for each individual model, the door to the agency opens, and a young woman walks in.

"Hey Arpi." Keri says. "Here to check on your numbers?"

Arpi Tahmasian is a 24 year old woman of Armenian descent, and the agency's most profitable model. Of the $7+ million cleared in the last quarter, Arpi brought in $3.8M of it. Her creamy skin is flawless, hair jet black, hanging laser straight down to her buttocks; her big deep brown eyes are hypnotic, and her frame is perfectly proportioned, 36-24-36 at 5' 6" tall. She is bilingual, yet she speaks English without a single hint of her native accent.

"No, not right now." Arpi answers. "I'm actually hoping to get a certain e-mail today."

"Today?" Keri asks. "On a Sunday?"

"Business waits for no one my friend." Arpi answers. "Not even on a Sunday. I've been on the phone all weekend with these guys, and I think we are now on the same page."

She minimizes Keri's window on the computer and signs into her company e-mail. She checks her inbox and finds what she is looking for. After reading the letter, she pumps her arm in jubilation.

"YES!" Arpi exclaims. "We got the contract, and I get a healthy cut."

"What contract?" Keri asks. "What have you been scheming?"

"Raylene's been trying to get this done for months now." Arpi replies. "The auto show circuit is coming around in four weeks, and Ray has been trying to get Ford Motors to use our models to pose with and present their Lincoln luxury line. When they were reluctant, she sent me as a living example of her 'product,' and they opened price negotiations."

"So we got the deal?" Keri asks.

"No only that," Arpi continues, "but while I was in Detroit, I also met secretly with low level GM and Fiat executives. GM agreed to use our girls for their Buick and Cadillac brands, and this e-mail from Fiat just informed me that we got Chrysler and Dodge. So instead of representing two brands over 12 months for $2.1 million, we get five brands for 12 months, for a total of $27.8 million, and since I brokered the deal, I wrote in a 10 percent cut for myself. That's $2.8 million in my pocket by mid-summer of next year. Damn, I'm good!"

"Oh my God!" Keri exclaims. "$27.8M for just one year? That's more than we pulled in for the last four!"

"Just wait until I tell Mom." Arpi exclaims. "She'll flip her lid."

"How many more girls will we have to recruit and sign in order to meet these contracts?" Keri asks.

"None." Arpi answers. "We have enough to meet the contracts now. So Ray can still recruit the additional girls she wants, and still be able meet our current and rising demand."

The phone rings.

"Oh." Keri says a bit surprised. "I thought the phones were turned off on Sundays."

"Nah," Arpi says, "most people tend to not call on Sundays, assuming we won't answer."

"Well," Keri replies, "let's hope this is more good news."

She answers the phone.

"Femme-Jolies Los Angeles." She says. "This is Keri, how may I help you?"

"Hi, good afternoon." The female caller says. "I'm a little surprised someone was there to pickup today."

"Business waits for no one my friend." Keri replies. "Not even on a Sunday. What can I do for you?"

Keri and Arpi share a silent chuckle.

"Well," the caller says, "I'm not to sure on how to go about this, but I heard that this is the premier agency in the Western United States. I've done some shoots in Oregon with Jean-Philippe Aristide, and I was about to sign with him, but I believe I have what it takes to work for Femmes-Jolies."

"Chasing your model dream in Los Angeles?" Keri asks. "Well you called the right place, we are the best. But you must understand that we only work with the best. You believe you have what it takes huh?"

"Absolutely I do!" The caller exclaims. "I was hoping to get an appointment with a photographer to do a trial shoot."

"There are a few steps we have to take before we do a screening." Keri replies.

Arpi quickly waves her hands to draw Keri's attention.

"One moment please." Keri says to the caller and places her on hold.

"This girl wants a screening?" Arpi asks. "Bring her in."

"But you know the protocol." Keri protests. "We have to see her photos first and then…"

"I'll see her myself." Arpi interrupts. "I'm a great judge of talent and character, and Mom trusts me. Give her to me, tomorrow at 3:30pm.

Keri sighs, then resumes her conversation with the caller.

"I'm sorry about the hold ma'am." She says. "Here's what we can do. Before we set you up with a photographer, we will want you to meet with one of our talent scouts. Her name is Arpi

Tahmasian and she will be available tomorrow at 3:30pm. This could be a once in a lifetime opportunity, can you make it?"

"Yes I can." The caller says.

"Can I have your name please?" Keri asks.

"Gloria Rolle." The caller says.

"Ok Ms. Rolle, we will see you tomorrow at 3:30pm." Keri says.

"Ok.' Gloria says. "Thank you, bye"

Natalie hangs up the phone and sits on the bed. So far, everything is going smoothly. The ultimate result is beyond her control. She will be there on time. Whether or not her mother would accept her, is another matter. The afternoon turns to evening, and Natalie decides to retire for the night. She must be restful, as tomorrow will be an eventful day.

Seven o'clock Monday morning, and the Santa Monica Pier is alive with activity. The end of the pier is closed to the public as photographers and set designers arrange the set for an important photo shoot. Femmes-Jolies is about to secure a 12-page spread for one of its models with a popular international men's magazine. The model in question is Isabella De Oro, and before she can land the shoot, she has to shine in her current assignment for a women swimwear designer. A makeshift changing room was constructed next to the set, and Isabella sits inside; a nervous wreck.

Isabella is a natural beauty with a slender waistline and voluptuous curves. Her olive skin tone is further enhanced by her hazel eyes and dark auburn tresses. Her 38" legs made her desirable in any shoot and situation. She considers herself lucky to be a model considering her past.

Isabella was not a bright student growing up, and dropped out of High School as a freshman. Her parents never pushed education, as her father was a partner in the largest oil company in all of Mexico. All she had to do was be smart enough to sign a contract to accept her inheritance.

That all changed two years ago. She became addicted to cocaine at age 16. When she was 17, she was arrested and sentenced to 4 months in rehab. After her time was completed, she was sent to spend 7 days in prison. Her incarceration proved to be a stain on her father's good name, and he banished her after her release. With nothing but the clothes on her back, she began to wander the streets. She went to a friend's house to stay, but was turned away.

That same night, a limousine pulled up along side of her. Inside, was a popular comedian. He believed she was a hooker and offered her $500 for sex. In desperate need of money, she accepted and went to a sleazy hotel with him. After the ordeal was over, she laid in bed and cried, unable to cope with her situation. The comedian thought she was dynamite and asked her to come on the road with his as his 'personal assistant.' She knew she would be used for sex, but felt she had not other choice, and accepted.

She was on tour with him for twelve weeks. During that time, drugs such as cocaine and marijuana were passed around freely, and she was passed from person to person in his entourage for their own sexual pleasure. She was paid $500 for each encounter and amassed a good amount of money, but it was all at the expense of her dignity. She cried herself to sleep every night. After seven weeks, she fled in the middle of the night. She took her saving of funds, approximately $14,000, and bought clothes, food, and rented an apartment. She set out one night in an attempt to reclaim her life, and fortune smiled on her. She was able to sneak into a political fundraising party and mingle with members of the Hollywood celebrity elite. During this party, she ran into Raylene Cordova, the founder and president of Femmes-Jolies Models Management.

Raylene thought Isabella was the most beautiful girl in the gathering and introduced herself. The two women spoke long into the night and Isabella was invited for a screening for the agency. On the day of the shoot, she was a nervous wreck, and worried she would blow her chance. In an attempt to calm her nerves, she snorted a line of cocaine. Her shoot was flawless and Raylene signed her to a contract before the photos were even developed.

Raylene discovered Isabella's addiction soon afterwards and insisted she return to rehab, courtesy of the agency. After her second stint in rehab, demand for Isabella flourished, and she was flown around the country for numerous requests. She was contacted by a lingerie company, wanting her image in their winter catalog. This shoot was a tremendous failure and she knew it. She went back to the dressing room and cried like she never cried before.

Raylene was not ready to give up on the opportunity. She was able to get Isabella a second chance that same day, then went to see her. As she cried, Raylene sat down next to her and hugged her. She then grabbed a small mirror and withdrew a small vial from around her neck. She opened the vial and poured the contents in one straight line on the mirror. It was half a gram of cocaine. Isabella looked at Raylene, confused. Raylene only nodded and handed Isabella a twenty dollar bill. Isabella took it, quickly rolled it and snorted the powder. She felt ashamed immediately afterwards, and looked at Raylene as if to apologize. Raylene drew her close and embraced her tightly, and whispered to her:

"Our little secret."

This shoot is no different. Isabella sits in the dressing room fidgeting in her chair. She knows she has to do well in order to get that spread, but she never responds well under pressure. She rubs her arms, her legs shake, and she hyperventilates. Her makeup has been perfected, but she is starting to sweat. She cannot get herself together.

She looks herself in the mirror and tries to convince herself, that she can do this clean, that she does not need the cocaine to get through this shoot, but with each passing minute, the tremors get worse. She can feel the tears well in her eyes as she knows she has no control over her cravings. She wants to scream, but she saves her strength, as Raylene enters the room.

Raylene takes a seat next to her prize pupil and smiles sweetly. She reaches over into her lap, grabs her hands and squeezes them lovingly, gently. Isabella returns the squeeze.

"I need you Izzy." Raylene says gently. "We need you. Me, the agency, the girls; we all need you to come through for us."

"I know Ray." Izzy replies. "I don't want to let you down."

"You won't." Raylene says. "You never have."

"I just wish it wasn't so hard." Izzy says meekly.

"What can I do for you?" Raylene asks. "What do you need from me?"

Isabella does not answer. Instead she looks Raylene in the eye, and then averts her gaze sadly to the floor. Raylene knows what that means. She slowly grabs her neck chain and withdraws the attached pendant from under her blouse. The pendant is a small vial. She unscrews the top and pours a small amount of white powder in a line on the vanity top. Isabella begins to cry and tries to cover her face.

"Izzy," Raylene says. "It's your choice. Whatever you choose, I'm here for you, and I love you."

Isabella wipes the tears from her eyes. Knowing she can not resist, she reaches for a straw, sticks it in her nose and snorts the cocaine. After the line is finished, she throws her head back and cries again. Raylene reaches over and pulls Isabella close to her and embraces the shivering girl. Isabella hugs back and cries into Raylene's shoulder.

"After we get the spread," Isabella says, "and finish it, I want to go back to rehab."

"Anything you need child." Raylene replies. "Mama's here for you."

The leave the dressing room and commence with the shoot.

Back at the agency, everything remains quiet. Keri is back at her desk going over the financials, and Arpi is in a talent recruitment meeting with the lead photographers. Nine o'clock rolls around, and the agency wild child comes to work. Willow Carter heads straight for the dressing room.

"WHASSUP BITCHES!!" She yells.

All heads turn towards Willow and greetings are exchanged.

"It's a beautiful fucking day in this beautiful fucking city." She continues, "and I'm ready to take some beautiful fucking pictures!"

Willow takes her seat next to her best friend in the agency, Hera Williams.

Hera was born in the Nigerian capital of Abuja to an American father and Nigerian mother. The family moved to the United States when Hera was just and infant, to escape the war and economic strife. When she was eight years old, her father was killed during a bank robbery while trying to protect an elderly woman, and Hera's mother raised her on her own since then. Through her mother, she learned to understand the value of hard work, respect, and education. She graduated from her High School as Valedictorian, and from UCLA, Magna Cum Laude. Aside from working as a model, she is still in school pursuing her Masters Degree in Organizational Development, with intentions on a Doctorate. She is six feet tall with dark chocolate skin, and short black hair with a perfect body.

"Is it at all possible for you to tone it down a bit?" Hera asks Willow.

"Hell fucking no!" Willow answers. "I am feeling too damn good!"

"Ah, and what's the cause of your jubilation?" Hera asks curiously.

"I got fucked last night!" Willow blurts loudly.

Brushes drop all over the room and everyone's head turns.

"Willow!" Hera shoots back. "You should keep your personal affairs to yourself!"

"Yes I should," Willow replies, "but I can't help it. For once, Ben did it right.

Hera's interest is now piqued.

"He's had problem before?" She asks.

"Oh yeah!" Willow answers. "Going too fast, moving too slow, finding the wrong hole, cumming before I did, he just could not get it right."

"He was that bad?" Hera inquires.

"Hell yeah." Willow answers. "Last month, for his birthday, I thought I'd do something nice for him, so I gave him head. You know what he does?"

"Do I really want to know?" Hera asks.

"Fuckin' A!" Willow replies. "He pops his fucking nuts off in my mouth!"

The entire dressing room falls into a stunned silence, although some girls giggle.

"I was so fucking pissed," Willow bellowed, "I got off my knees, and spit it right back in his face!"

"So I assume he was better last night." Hera says.

"Oh yes." Willow replies happily. "Much better. Oh God, I lost track of how many time I came, but he did his job."

"I also assume you are ready for the import tuner shoot you're scheduled to do." Hera says.

Willow jumps out of her seat.

"AH!" She yells. "FUCK ME!"

She bolts for the main office.

In the main office, Arpi sits at the desk, going over the terms of the new contract and congratulating herself. She is about to print the contracts and stage them for Raylene to find, when Willow burst in.

"Who the fuck is booking me to pose with fucking rice rockets?" Willow demands.

"Good morning to you too sis." Arpi replies.

"I hate those fucking things!" Willow asks. "Do I look like a little Asian schoolgirl to you?"

"You're asking the wrong person." Arpi answers. "Your shoot this morning was Mama Ray's call, not mine."

"No." Willow barks. "No, no, no! That's impossible. Mama Ray knows that I have an exclusivity clause with American Muscle Revival Magazine. You know, Mustangs, GTOs, Firebirds, and shit. If I'm caught flashing my cooch on the hood of a RX7 or some other Asian or Euro shit, I'll lose my publication bonus. I ain't gonna fucking let that happen."

Arpi clicks the print icon on the computer and the printer roars to life.

"If I were you," Arpi begins, "I wouldn't worry about it too much."

She pulls the document off the printer and hands it to Willow.

"What's this?" Willow asks.

"It a contract." Arpi says. "I contract that makes us the exclusive provider of models for the international car show circuit for the Chrysler group. And, I'll give you three guesses as to who they want to introduce their latest Dodge pony car to the public."

Willow's eyes shoot up excitedly.

"Really?" She squeals. "Sis, you're the best!"

She throws her arms around Arpi and squeezes her tightly. Arpi reciprocates. After a few seconds, Willow releases her grip.

"I swear," Willow says with a tear rolling down her face. "You must be my guardian angel."

Arpi and Willow did not grow up together, but they do have a history. Arpi was a solid student, and was studying to be a pediatrician. During her internship at County USC Hospital, she was called in to help with an underage attempted rape victim. The girls was not raped, but was very traumatized and the hospital wanted to be sure she was not hurt. Arpi became emotional attached to the young girl and came to think you her like a little sister. The hospital felt she crossed an emotional line, jeopardizing her judgment as a doctor, and she was released from the program. The young girl was Willow Carter.

Willow Carter began life as a pacifist child. She was not socially active, not popular in school, and refused to let anyone get to know her. One day when she was 14 years old, she was walking home from school, when she was pulled into an alley. An attacker threw her to the ground and held a knife to her throat. Willow just reacted. She had enough space to drive her knee into his groin and she fought for the knife. In the struggle, she was punched and struck multiple times, but she never relented. She was thrown back to the ground and the man pulled out a gun. She fought for this weapon as well. He fell on top of her and a bullet was fired, piercing his heart and killing him. She laid there crying hysterically while her dead attacker bled all over her. She used her cell phone to call 911, and begged for help in the aftermath.

While in the hospital, she met and befriended Arpi, who never left her alone, and would always check on her at night, sometimes going as far as sleeping in her room so she would not feel alone. After Willow was discharged, Arpi was dismissed from duty. When Willow returned home, she vowed never to be a victim again and she changed everything about her. She became a rebel, covering herself in tattoos and piercings, and getting into fights at school. While still considered a social outcast, it was a title she now revered and preferred.

Four years passed, and Arpi was fully entrenched with Femmes-Joiles. She was out having lunch one day when she saw two girls fighting in an alley. Against her better judgment, she ran in to break it up, and was struck in the face. She fell down and one of the girls ran off. The other approached Arpi, ready to confront her when both girls froze. The remaining girl was Willow, and she remembered Arpi, as the caring nurse in the hospital. Arpi never forgot about her and stared in amazement. Willow began to cry tears of joy at the impromptu reunion and they embraced. Arpi, on a whim, took Willow to the agency. Raylene had a need for a girl with a hard punk edge and signed Willow to a contract immediately.

"You guys better have an awesome explanation as to why Willow is not at her shoot." A female voice rang out.

Breaking their embrace, Arpi and Willow look at the door. Standing there as an imposing figure, is Raylene. She is pleased to see her girls hugging, but troubled that Willow is not getting ready for her shoot.

"Mom!" Both girls squeal simultaneously.

They both run over and hug Raylene. She can't help but smile.

"Willow my dear," Raylene says, "why are you not at hair and makeup? You only have an hour until the shoot."

"You know the stipulation with AMR mom." Willow shoots back. "I'll lose my bonus if I pose with imports."

"I am fully aware of that fact." Raylene replies, "but they low balled us on that deal, and this could twist their arm into a revision. Besides, the import spread requested you directly."

"What if we came upon a small financial windfall within the next five minutes?" Arpi interrupted. "Would she have to go then?"

Raylene shoots a glance at her prized model.

"What do you mean?" She asked.

Arpi goes back to the printer and takes out the printed contracts. She straightens them and hands them to Raylene. The boss puts her glasses on and read over the details in the first contract. She lowers the papers and stares at Arpi.

"How do you plan on presenting this to GM in the next five minutes?" She asks.

"I don't have to." Arpi answers. "Last week, when you sent me to Detroit, I got Ford, but I also met with GM and Fiat. They agreed to my terms, our terms. They want to use us, and all you have to do is sign."

"What are the financials?" Raylene asks.

"$27.8 million," Arpi answers, "with the potential for a multi-year deal after this year."

She reaches to the desk for a pen and hands it to Raylene.

"You brokered the deal?" Raylene asks. "What's your cut?"

"Ten percent." Arpi answers. "Annually."

Raylene cannot hold her stern stare and chuckles at the girls.

"What didn't you tell me about this earlier?" She asks.

"Um," Arpi begins, "happy birthday?"

Raylene laughs and reaches out to hug Arpi. Willow joins in the hug.

"So," Raylene says, "I guess you're off the hook for now Willow."

"Damn right!" Willow replies.

"Oh, before I forget," Raylene cuts in. "Ben is in the waiting room."

"What the fuck does he want?" Willow asks.

"I'm sure he probably wants to see you." Raylene answers.

"Fuck me!" Willow exclaims.

She steps away from the women and leaves the office. Raylene looks at Arpi and hugs her again.

"I love you so much my dear." She says.

"I love you too mom." Arpi replies.

They break their embrace.

"I always love it when you call me that." Raylene says. "It just sounds so right coming from you."

"Oh!" Arpi squeals. "You're gonna make me cry."

She blushes and hides her face in her hands.

"I mean it." Raylene continues. "Domi is my precious little princess, and you are her big sister. The oldest daughter I've always wanted. So much more than Natal…." Her voice trails off.

Her smile drops and her stare becomes blank.

"So much more than what?" Arpi asks.

Raylene snaps back to reality.

"Oh, um, nothing." She responds. "I'm just, going off on a tangent. Let's just say, you make me forget about all the mistakes I've ever made in the past."

"Thanks mom." Arpi replies.

Willow makes her way slowly down the hall towards the waiting room. As she enters, she scans the room and finds Ben.

Benjamin Spence is a rookie police officer. At 20 years old, he is two years older than Willow, but in their relationship, he is submissive to her. She is rude, bossy, and sometimes cruel, yet he has strong feeling for her and believes he can get her to feel the same way. Because of his relationship with Willow, Raylene uses him as a bodyguard, despite his klutziness.

"What the fuck are you doing here?" She asks.

"Hey baby." He says.

He jumps out his seat tries to rush over to her, but trips over his own feet and lands on his face. Willow lowers her head in shame.

"What do you want?' She asks.

"I just wanted to see you." He answers. "You know, see how you're doing this morning."

"I'm fine." She shoots back. "Bye."

As she turns to walk away, he gets up and grabs her by the shoulder.

"Hey, hey wait." He says. "Is that it? You're not happy to see me?"

"Should I be?" She asks.

"It's just that," He answers, "you know, I thought we bonded last night."

"Bonded?" She asks. "Um, yes bonded. Your cock, my cunt, you call it bonding, I call it fucking. Yes, we bonded last night, but we've bonded before, so why should this time be any different?"

"It's just um," He answers, "last night I thought you finally connected with me."

"Yes I connected," She replies, "but that was my first connection with you, and it takes more than one night of mind-blowing connections to mean anything."

She turns to leaves again, he does not stop her.

"When can we see each other again?" He asks.

"I'll let you know!" she says as she leaves.

Before she disappears around the corner, she steals one last glance at him and shoots him a flirtatious wink. He smiles in response. After she is gone, he jumps for joy and pumps his fist, striking the low hanging light fixture and shattering glass all over the floor. Embarrassed, he looks to see if anyone saw him and finds Keri silently laughing behind the reception desk.

"Tell Ray I'll pay for that." He says sheepishly.

Two o'clock in the afternoon and Natalie is in a cab, headed for the Femme-Jolies Modeling Agency. She did not sleep the previous night, and her nerves are shot. Seven years have passed since she last saw her or even heard from her mother and she did not know what to expect. She hopes to be accepted, but is trying to prepare to be rejected. She looked at the website again and noticed how a few model called her 'Mama Ray,' meaning she acted like a mother figure to them; quite the opposite of how she treated Natalie. She hopes this meant a transformation occurred in her mother and she would welcome back her daughter.

The taxi arrives at the Twin Towers in Century City at 2:43 pm. Natalie pays the faire and the driver leaves. Natalie takes one last cleansing breathe and walks into the East building. She finds the concierge and asks how to get to the agency. He tells her it is on the 40th floor of the West tower. She thanks him and heads to the other tower. Once inside, she makes her way to the elevator, presses the up button and waits. The elevator opens and people file out. Most are talking on cell phones, and all are dressed in fine business suits. As these people leave, Natalie and a group of other people pile on.

The ride to the 40th floor is hot, crammed, and stuffy. The elevator stops at seven different floors before reaching the 40th. Exiting the elevator, Natalie checks the time; 2:53 pm. She scuttles off to the bathroom to fix her shuffled clothes. In the bathroom, she looks in the mirror and is disgusted. She feels she is hiding who she truly is, and reverting back to her victim mentality. She wants to let her personality hang out. Hastily, she removes her sweater and throws it in the trash, leaving only her halter top. She gives her hair a quick toss and takes her belt off. Looking in the mirror, she feels much better now and smiles. She leaves and heads for the suite.

Keri sits at her desk and inputs the information from Arpi's latest contract acquisitions into her computer at the reception desk. She wants to finish early so she can take an early lunch. As she punches in the final details, the suite door opens and a young woman walks in. She is slightly taller than average height with long flowing blond hair and a toned body. Keri sees girls like this come in everyday, and is not surprised by this one. She puts on her best face and greets the visitor.

"Good Afternoon." Keri says. "Welcome to Femmes-Jolies Los Angeles. Do you have an appointment?"

"Yes I do." The woman says in a friendly tone. "I'm here to see Arpi Tahmasian for a 3:30pm interview."

"Ah yes," Keri exclaims, "Miss Gloria Rolle. We've been anxiously waiting to meet you. Arpi is in a meeting with management, but she should be out in time. Feel free to wait here while she concludes her business. She will be right with you."

"Thank you very much." The woman says.

Natalie leaves the reception desk and heads for a chair. She picks up a magazine and begins to read it. After ten minutes of waiting, a woman's voice can be heard. She sounds like she is on a cell phone and her language is very profane. The woman walks into the waiting room, and Natalie, actually feels a little star struck. It was Willow Carter.

"Fuck those French Bitches!" She blurts into the phone. "What the fuck does a Frenchie know about bars and road houses? Jack shit, that's what!"

Willow roams randomly around the waiting room, never missing a beat of her prolonged conversation. Natalie watches in amazement.

I like her, but how can she be a model?

Natalie sees the many tattoos, and no attempt to hide them. Small ones covered her arms and legs, a big one settled in the middle of her back, and a tear drop was tattooed under her left eye. She listens to her conversation and marvels at how she does not hold back.

Natalie decides to make contact, but Willow looks unapproachable. She decided to use the best ice breaker she has.

She gets up and walks to the table across the room. She squats down and pretends to flip through the magazines on the table. Her halter top rides up slightly, fully exposing the black widow on her back. Within seconds, Willow takes notice.

"Killer tat!" Willow yells.

Natalie looks over her shoulder and smiles at Willow.

"I'll call you back." Willow says and hangs up the phone.

"Nice isn't it?" Natalie asks.

"Fucking sweet!" Willow answers. "Where'd you get that?"

"Back in my hometown in Oregon." Natalie answers.

"Who pissed you off so bad?" Willow asks.

"Don't know what you're talking about." Natalie replies.

"Don't give me that bullshit." Willow responds. "No one gets a tat that aggressive without a story behind it. The way I see it, some bitch claiming to be the Queen Bee, royally pissed you off, and you did something about it. Judging by that design, you either whooped that pretty ass or you killed her. So don't bullshit me. What's the bitch's name?"

Natalie chuckles lightly.

"Heather." Natalie says. "The bitch's name is Heather."

"That has got to be, like, the number one bitch name of all time." Willow says. "When have you ever met a Heather that you didn't just wanna skullfuck with a tire iron?"

"Um," Natalie mumbles, "You know, I really can't recall."

Willow gives a light chuckle of her own.

"So what'd you do to her?" Willow asks. "You whoop that sweet ass?"

"Actually," Natalie answers, "I broke her neck with the blunt end of a hammer, paralyzing her. Then I buried her alive."

"Nice," Willow exclaims, "I'm scared of you."

"You should be." Natalie replies.

"So what's your name bitch?" Willow asks.

"Natal…" Natalie begins, but cuts herself off. "…Gloria Rolle."

Natal…Gloria Rolle?" Willow asks. "Call me crazy, but I think you're hiding something."

Natalie has to think fast.

"My first name by birth is Natalya." Natalie lies. "My father named me, but he was abusive to my mom, so I try not to use it."

"Well, Gloria," Willow says. "I'm Willow Carter. Who are you here to see?"

"Arpi Tahmasian." Natalie answers. "I have an appointment at 3:30pm."

"So you've already done the screening then?" Willow asks.

"Not yet." Natalie answers. "I just got into town yesterday, called and this is whom someone matched me up with."

"Well, I'll tell you what Gloria." Willow says. "I'm gonna tag along on this appointment 'cuz I like ya. Arpi's like my big sister, and if I green light you, she will too."

As if on cue Arpi enters the room and approaches the two women. She extends her hand to Natalie.

"Hello there." She says. "You must be Gloria. I'm Arpi, and I see you've met Willow."

"Yes I have." Natalie says.

Willow throws her arm around Natalie's shoulders.

"This girl fucking rocks!" She says. "She's just like me."

"Well," Arpi says, "an endorsement from one of our favorite models is always a good thing. Please follow me Miss Rolle."

The three girls leave the waiting room and head to a conference room down the hall. They sit close together and begin a conversation.

"Over the phone," Arpi begins, "you mentioned that you heard we were the best in the Western United States. Do you know anything about our founder?"

MOTHER!

"Yes," Natalie answers, "a little bit. The agency was founded about four to five years ago by Raylene Cordova, a former fashion model. She left her hometown after she decided to quit modeling and started this agency."

"Yes." Arpi replies. "She was quite a runway icon back in her day, walking the runways in Paris and Milan by age fourteen. I think the most amazing thing about her is that she decided to leave the industry when she was twenty years old. She was on the top of her game, and she just walked away. She re-emerged 13 years later in Los Angeles and this is what has become of it."

Natalie grows sick to her stomach listening to this girl spewing praise about her mother. She fights the urge to vomit and presses forward with the interview.

"Will we be seeing this amazing woman today?" Natalie asks.

"Probably not," Arpi says, "but she is in the suite, and we might run into her. So Gloria, what could you bring to this agency?"

"I can bring anything you need Arpi." Natalie answers. "You ladies look like excellent judges of talent, why don't you tell me, where you see me fitting."

"I told you this bitch was just like me." Willow says. "Don't you just love her?"

Arpi laughs quietly.

"Gloria," Arpi says, "your body is amazing! Obviously you've put a lot of work into it. Your face is angelic, yet I detect a hint of a rough edge with you. I think Ray would love you. What do you say Willow?"

"Definitely." Willow exclaims. "Can't you just picture me and her posing for Dodge? That would be killer!"

"Just what I was thinking." Arpi replies. "Here's what we'll do. We'll tour the sets and the costumes today, just to give you feel of how we do things here. Then, we'll setup a screening for you tomorrow. Two shoots, one with you solo, and one with you and Willow. Should those go well, we will setup a final meeting with Raylene that afternoon."

"Sounds good." Natalie says.

"Good." Arpi responds. "Let's go walk the sets."

The girls leave the conference room and head to the first set. A young woman is modeling clothes on an Italian motif. Arpi explains the concept and inspirations for the shoot. She also details the clients and the expected results.

They leave the first set and head to a second. This time, the motif is Japanese and an Asian girl models with an Asian male. Again, Arpi explains the purpose of and inspiration behind the shoot, expectations and client details. They get ready to leave the set and head to the final set.

BAM!

A person carrying a stack of papers and boxes walks right into Natalie, knocking them both over and spilling the papers all over the floor. Natalie sits up straight and sees the mess all around her. Out of reflex she starts scooping the papers, helping the person pick them up.

"Doesn't anyone watch were they are going anymore?" The person says.

Natalie freezes. She has heard that voice before, but it was so long ago. It is a woman's voice, and it chills her to the bone. Slowly Natalie raises her head to see the person. Her face is not visible as she is scooping papers. Her hair is blond and her frame is very thin. She mumbles as she works to clean up the mess. She looks up to see who she ran into, and she too, freezes.

Mother and Daughter stare at each other, face to face, and neither one blinks. Natalie can hardy believe her eyes. This is the first time she has seen her mother since she dropped her off at Nana's house seven years ago, and she looks exactly the same. Her emotions go crazy. She is torn between wanting to run away, wanting to break down and cry, and wanting to lash out. Her thoughts race and she cannot move.

Raylene is just as confused. What should a happy moment, causes her pain, uneasiness and guilt. She has never seen this woman before, but she is certain that this woman was the girl whom she left all those years ago. She cried herself to sleep for a year after she left Natalie with her grand-mother, but then never mentioned her name to anyone. For the first time since she came to Los Angeles, she did not know what to do. Emotion made her speak first.

"Natalie?" She asks in a shaky voice.

"Mom?" Natalie asks back.

The set stops in its tracks, and every head turned to the unfolding scene. Raylene never spoke of Natalie to anyone, even to her favorite confidant Arpi. Willow and Arpi for their part, are stunned. Staring hard, they can now see the resemblance and the confusion grows.

"Oh my God, Natalie." Raylene says.

Emotion makes Natalie react. She slowly reaches out her hand and touches her mother's shoulder. Raylene jumps back.

"No!" She shouts.

She shoots to her feet.

"No." She says again, "It can't…you're….Natalie….Oh my God. Natalie…no."

She covers her mouth and runs away.

"MOM!" Natalie yells behind her. "Please don't leave me again!"

Raylene stops in the doorway. With tears running down her face, she stares at her crying daughter. She cannot stand the sight and runs off.

Natalie is heartbroken. When they locked eyes, she could not help but hope that this would be a new beginning for her. Instead, she was shunned and rejected by her own mother yet again. She cannot stand being in this place any longer, so she gets up and darts out of the set and leaves the agency.

Raylene reaches her office and slams the door shut. She opens her hutch behind the desk, takes out a decanter of bourbon, pours some into a glass, and drinks it quickly. When she finishes the drink, she throws the glass onto the floor, shattering it.

"DAMMIT!" She screams.

"Mom!" a voice yells at her.

"No!" Raylene screams back.

She looks up and sees Arpi poking her head into the office. Raylene slinks into her office chair, lowers her head and begins to cry. Arpi walks in and kneels next to her, trying to provide comfort.

"Is it true?" She asks softly.

Raylene cannot answer. She can only nod her head yes. Arpi grabs her hand and gives it a squeeze.

"Oh, Mom." She says.

"It was 19 years ago." Raylene tearfully begins. "I was just a 20 year old kid. I was in London, desperately trying to land a contract. I went to a screening and gave them everything I had. A week had past, and I heard nothing back. I cried my heart out, and my mother walked in on me. She told me, that tears won't get me the work. I had to go out and get it, no matter what the consequences. A few days later, I ran into the photographer, Alphonse Parrish. I made idle chat with him, and convinced him to give me a private shoot in his studio that afternoon. I seduced him, hoping to gain some influence him with to persuade the talent scouts. However, more months passed, and I found out I was pregnant. I was beginning to show when they finally called me back, offering me a contract. Once I got to the office, they saw I was pregnant and rescinded the offer. I attacked Alphonse, scarring him badly and ruining my reputation. I wasn't able to find work in the industry after that."

Arpi hangs on every word, never interrupting.

"I returned to America," Raylene continues, "where my mother promptly put me out, saying I was a failure. Taking the money I had in savings, I moved to Oregon. Real estate was cheap, so I could afford to buy a nice house and pay cash for it. I had the baby, but didn't even have a name for her. Shit, I pulled the name Natalie out of thin air. I tried to get back in the game afterward, but no one would hire me. If it were not for the trademarks of my name and images, I would have gone broke and starved. I felt my life was ruined, and I blamed Natalie for it. I thought, maybe if I got her in the industry, then I could get it back, but she was so resistant. She was a shy child, very closed off, and would not work to improve herself. She came home from school everyday complaining about bullies, but I knew it was because, she didn't apply herself. Every time I looked at her, I saw the life I lost, the life I once had, and it drove me insane. After 12 years, I couldn't take it anymore. I took Natalie to her grandmother's house and left for Los Angeles. Today was the first time I've seen her since then."

"Why didn't you tell us?" Arpi asks.

"What would you have done?" Raylene asks back. "Begged me to go back and get her? I left her there to have a better life than what I could've given her. I was prepared to live with my shame, and let her live her life."

"But she's back now." Arpi interjects. "What're you going to do?"

Before she can answer, Willow burst into the room.

"That lying bitch!" She exclaims. "She lied to us to reconnect with her mother? God, I love that!"

"Willow!" Arpi yells. "Now is not the time!"

"Oh yeah!" Willow blurts.

She runs over to Raylene and throws her arms around her.

"How you doing Mom?" Willow asks.

The candor makes Raylene smile.

"Better," She answers, "now that you girls are here."

"What're you gonna do Ray?" Arpi asks again.

"Nothing." Raylene answers. "I just can't handle all this right now."

"C'mon Mom." Willow protests. "Bring her back. You saw how broken up she was. She really does miss you. She wouldn't have come all the way from Oregon is she didn't think…."

"How'd you know where she came from?" Raylene demands.

"We were talking in the waiting room." Willow answers. "She has this killer tat…."

"You knew she was here?" Raylene shouts. "Why didn't you come get me?"

"She used a fake name Mom." Arpi interjects. "We had no idea."

"You were there too?" Raylene yells.

"Take it easy chica!" Willow replies.

"No!" Raylene shouts. "I will not take it easy. You two let a girl in here using a fake name and I'm supposed to take it easy? How can you be so irresponsible? I'm very disappointed in the both of you, especially you Arpi."

The directness of her remarks stings Arpi and keeps her silent.

"Leave me alone." Raylene continues. "Both of you, go now."

The girls do not protest and head towards the door leading to the hallway. Willow exits first. Before Arpi leaves, she turns to face her crying boss.

"You know what Ray?" She asks. "If you are reacting this way towards your own daughter, how will you treat us if something goes wrong here?"

She exits the office and joins Willow in the hallway.

"I'd be worried if Domi ever got a bad grade in school." Willow says.

"C'mon." Arpi says. "Let's go."

"Where are we going?" Willow asks.

"Just shut up and get your car keys." Arpi answers. "You're driving."

Back in her hotel room, Natalie sits on her bed with her face buried in her hands, crying her eyes out. She knows she should not be surprised. She knows her mother is cruel, heartless, and cared for no one but herself. Despite this, a small part of Natalie hoped to be accepted, and welcomed into her mother's arms. She wanted to feel the warmth of a motherly hug, and perhaps be loved. As her mind races she cannot focus herself.

Rejected again!

Rejection is never easy to take, and this time was no different. She knows her Mother hates her, and this afternoon just confirmed that fact. She now has to figure out what to do next. Before she can formulate her thoughts, there is a loud knock on her door.

"Go away!" She yells.

Another knock.

"GO THE FUCK AWAY!" She screams.

Once again, the knock repeats at the door, pissing Natalie off. She jumps off the bed and pounds on the door in retaliation.

"I SAID GO AWAY!" She screams again.

"Natalie, please open up." A female voice pleads.

She recognizes the voice. Her anger subsides, but her curiosity piques. She undoes the lock and opens the door. She recognizes her visitors and stays silent.

Arpi and Willow stand on the other side of the door. They look at Natalie but are unsure of what to say to her.

"Whassup bitch." Willow says. She tries to sound playful, but Natalie can sense the trepidation in her voice.

"Hi Natalie." Arpi says gently.

Natalie's face is red and wet from her tears, but she tries to remain composed.

"Hi." Natalie replies.

"I know this is really awkward," Arpi says, "and I understand if you want to be alone so I'll…"

"No, no." Natalie interrupts. "Come in."

Natalie steps aside and the two young ladies enter the hotel room.

"How'd you guys locate me?" Natalie asks.

"You told us where you were staying," Arpi answers, "as we walked past the first set. You probably just don't remember."

Willow wraps her arms around Natalie and lays her head on her shoulder.

"You okay sweetie?" She asks.

"No." Natalie answers. "I'm not okay. How am I supposed to be okay when my Mom just rejects me? She abandoned me seven years ago, left me with that horrible woman, and she still wants nothing to do with me. What the fuck did I do that was so horrible, that she just wants to remove me from her life?"

"Maybe she just needs more time to get used to the idea." Arpi answers.

"Maybe she's just hard headed." Willow says.

"What?" Natalie asks.

"Think back to when you were young for a second." Willow replies. "Was Ray really stubborn about things?"

"Very stubborn." Natalie answers. "Everything had to be her way or the highway."

"Oh see Arpi." Willow responds. "Some things never change. She was always like this."

"Willow!" Arpi cuts in. "Not right now!"

"What not now?" Natalie asks. "What are you not telling me?"

Arpi sighs slightly.

"She is reluctant to do anything," she says, "in regards to your re-emergence. She'd rather imagine that it did not happen."

"Ain't that some bullshit?" Willow asks.

"Same old mom." Natalie replies.

"Natalie," Arpi says, "I know that you feel like…well, I have no idea how you feel, I can only imagine. But I do know that answers are not easy to come by. Although, Willow and I just met you, we want to be there for you. We want to help you."

"Help me do want?" Natalie asks. "Get psychiatric help as to why I have this strange need to feel accepted by a narcissistic bitch like my mother?"

"Actually," Arpi answers, "we were hoping we could help broker a healing and reunion for you, with your mother."

"Ha!' Natalie scoffs. "You saw how she reacted to me. It would take a miracle for her to change her tune."

"Good thing Arpi's a fucking Catholic then." Willow replies.

"Thank you." Arpi says sarcastically.

"What do you think you could do?" Natalie asks.

"Before we tell you," Arpi answers, "we need to know one thing. What's your story? What have you been doing all this time without Ray?"

Natalie takes a deep breath to clear her thoughts.

"Alot of crying." Natalie answers. "I just couldn't conform to the way she wanted me to be, to live, to behave. I hated the clothes, hated the attitudes, and hated the lifestyle. I tried to be my own person, but it was never good enough for her, or society. I had to deal with bullies and all their crap for years. After she left me, it was more of the same. One day, I decided that maybe, I just couldn't win. So I made the decision to change to the way Mom wanted me to be, hoping that one day, I would see her again. I even went to college last fall, but couldn't stay the whole semester because a killer got loose on campus."

"A killer got loose?" Arpi asks.

"Yeah." Natalie answers. "You may have heard about it. I went to Westin State University."

"You were there?" Willow shouts. "I followed that story on the social media. Six students and one cop were killed. One poisoned, one drowned, one stabbed to death, one ran down, and two were found dead at a construction site. The cop was killed with arrows right?"

"Yeah." Natalie confirms. "I started to fear for my safety, so I left. I knew that Mom was a model, so I tried to get into the business, hoping it would help me connect with her. Yesterday, I just left and came here, hoping a leap of faith would bring me to her."

"A leap of faith?" Willow asks. "Did I mention that Arpi is a fucking Catholic?"

"Willow that's enough!" Arpi says.

Willow leans in towards Natalie.

"She always gets touchy when I get on her for being Catholic." Willow says. "She must like little boys!"

Arpi takes a deep breath to calm her nerves.

"Anyway," She begins, "let me be 100% percent honest as to why we are here and offering to help you."

"Please, be honest." Natalie replies.

"There are three reasons." Arpi continues. "The first reason is personal. Raylene has done so much for us as models, we feel like reuniting her happily with her biological daughter would be a great thing for her."

"Okay." Natalie replies. "That's noble of you."

"The second reason," Arpi continues, "is professional. I meant what I said in the conference room, you are a knockout, and could be a very profitable asset to the agency, especially working in tandem with Willow. You could bring us millions of dollars per year and more money for the agency, means more money for us."

"Okay." Natalie replies.

"Final and most important reason," Arpi concludes, "is Dominique."

"Dominique?" Natalie asks. "Who's Dominique?"

Willow grabs Natalie's hand and holds it.

"Brace yourself sweetie." She says. "This is good news, but may be tough to take."

Arpi takes a deep cleansing breath.

"Dominique," Arpi continues, "is you baby sister."

"WHAT?" Natalie shouts.

"Five years ago," Arpi goes on, "Raylene and her fiancée had a daughter. You have a sister."

"Oh my God!" Natalie exclaims.

She shoots her hands to her face and gasps in disbelief. Her heart flutters and she goes into a blank state of mind. A tug of war ensues as different emotions fight for control over her mind. She wants to feel joy; the joy anyone would feel at gaining a younger sibling, yet she cannot help but feel that she has been replaced. Her silence is deafening.

"Natalie!" Willow interjects. "Say something bitch."

"Oh my God." Natalie repeats.

Tears stream down her face.

"I don't believe it." She says.

"Believe it." Arpi replies. "Despite how either you or Ray feels about this whole situation, Domi deserves to know the truth."

"Domi." Natalie says and cracks a small smile. "That sounds so cute."

"She's a cutie," Arpi says, "and she will flip when she finds out she has an older sister."

Natalie's joy subsides.

"That won't happen." She replies. "Mom has already rejected me once, there is no way she would welcome me into her life, and let me meet my sister."

"That's where we come in." Willow piques.

"How?" Natalie asks.

"Tomorrow night." Arpi answers. "Ray invited Willow and I, along with her two other favorite models Hera and Izzy, to her house to celebrate our new surge in business. We want to bring you with us."

"Why?" Natalie asks. "So she can cause a scene in front of more people?"

"While that would be hella cool," Willow answers, "we have different intentions."

"Being at her home would give you a captive audience with her." Arpi continues. "Willow and I would get everyone else out of the room, and you two could hash it out. Hopefully, by the end of the night, you guys can come to some sort of understanding, and begin healing."

"You think it'll work?" Natalie asks.

"We won't know unless we try." Arpi answers.

Natalie ponders the possibility for a moment. An audience with her mother could be the key to open communication. It could give her a chance to vent her frustrations, and finally bury her past. Her eyes well up in uncertainty, but she has to take a chance. Even if it did not work, maybe she can gain a foot hold, and slowly climb the ladder from there. She longed to connect with her mother, and saw her opportunities as fleeting. She takes a deep breath, and then looks Arpi in the eye.

"Let's do it." She says. "I'll take a shot."

"Good." Arpi replies and gives a smile.

"Alright." Willow interjects. "That's a good bitch."

"Why do you cuss so fucking much?" Natalie asks Willow sharply.

"What?" Willow replies. "Can't a bitch holla and speak her fucking mind?"

"You'll have to forgive Willow." Arpi cuts in. "That's just how she is, and there's no way around it."

"Damn straight!" Willow shoots back.

"Really?" Natalie asks.

"Yeah." Arpi answers. "Last month, she met the mayor and told him, 'Sorberé su pene verdadero bien para cinco dólares,'"

"What does that mean?" Natalie asks.

"Trust me," Arpi answers, "you don't want to know."

"All he had to say was 'Si,'" Willow says, "and a good time would have been had by all."

"Anyway," Arpi cuts in, "back to the topic at hand. We will pick up here, tomorrow night at 7:30 pm."

"I'll be ready." Natalie replies.

The girls stand up and head for the door. Arpi gives one last smile and shakes Natalie's hand. Willow does not settle for a handshake. She reaches over and gives Natalie a big hug, which is eagerly accepted.

"Worst case scenario," Willow says, "if this doesn't work, stick around town. You and I can kick it. I'll get you into this business one way or the other."

"Thank you." Natalie says graciously.

"Don't thank me ho," Willow shoots back, "I just want a ten percent cut of that ass!"

With that statement, she smacks Natalie on the backside and walks out the door.

"Woohoo! Go Team Ambush Reunion!" she yells as she walks down the hall.

Arpi glances at Natalie, silently apologizes, and follows Willow down the hall. After closing and locking the door, Natalie contemplates the arraignment for tomorrow, and for the first time in a while, she feels hopeful. This is the first time she can think of that anyone has come to her aid and offered to help her out with anything. She lies back on her bed tries to think positively.

Back in the hallway, Willow and Arpi wait for the elevator to arrive. Willow is smiling, pleased with the effort and compassion that she and Arpi have just shown. Arpi keeps a blank stare. Her intentions with this meeting were not for the sake of being kind. Natalie represented an uncontrollable variable in her otherwise perfect world. Depending how Raylene reacts to this situation, Arpi's business dealings could be adversely affected. If Raylene accepts Natalie, she might sign her to a contract and give her the highest paying clients and deals. Arpi cannot accept that. In her years of dealing with Raylene, she knows that the boss hates to feel as if she is being forced into a corner, and reacts accordingly. By forcing this meeting with Natalie, Arpi would further the rejection and reinforce her standing as Raylene's favorite and most profitable model. She could not tell Willow the truth or she would not have gone along with it. She hates lying to Willow, but this was not the first time, nor will it be the last.

Back at her home, Raylene is still a wreck. She has not taken any phone calls, nor has she spoken to anyone. She sits on her couch in her dark unlit living room and stares into the darkness. Every few minutes, she will take a swallow from a glass, containing straight, unmixed vodka.

After she dismissed Arpi and Willow, she headed home. When she arrived, she stared at the many pictures on her wall. Some of them were of her, Michael, and various friends. Most were of Dominique. She swelled with pride upon seeing those photos. Dominique brought her so much joy, she could not help but smile whenever she saw her. She stares at one particular photo of Dominique posing at Disneyland. She feels so happy, and tries to enjoy the feeling. When she closes her eyes however, she sees Natalie; angrily staring her down. She abruptly opens her eyes, desperate to shake the image, but she cannot. She grabs her hair and groans as the pressure builds in her head. She runs to the kitchen-side bar and retrieves a full bottle of Vodka. She turns off the lights and sits on her coach in darkness. Hours pass and her headache grows.

Michael Milton pulls into the driveway of the home he shares with his fiancée and daughter. It's late at night and he is very tired. He looks in his passenger seat and watches his daughter sleep next to him. He agreed to pick her up from school that afternoon, but was called back to his production studio. In a crunch for time, he took Dominique with him. She is a very well behaved child, so this was not a problem for him. When they got in the car, she nodded her head and slept for the 45 minute drive home. He reaches over and nudges her on her shoulder.

"Wake up sleeping beauty." He says.

She stirs slowly and groans. She opens her eyes and smiles when she sees her father.

"Are we home daddy?" She asks.

"Yes we are sweet pea." He answers. "Get you backpack."

She reaches behind her to the backseat and retrieves her backpack. She exits the passenger side door and waits for her dad. He comes around, grabs her hand and walks her to the front door. Michael feels some uneasiness, as all the lights are turned off. He slowly leads Domi to the front door, making sure she doesn't fall down and hurt herself. He unlocks the front door and turns on the entry light. The surroundings inside the house are all dark. He slowly makes his way to the living room and turns on the lights.

"No fucking lights!" Raylene yells.

"Raylene?" Michael asks.

Michael looks over to the couch and sees Raylene sitting there with her hands over her eyes. She struggles to see the area around her.

"Michael." She says. "What the hell do you want?"

"Mommy." Dominique says. "Those are naughty words."

"Then cover your fucking ears!" Raylene shoots back.

Michael quickly squats down to hold his trembling daughter.

"Daddy," Domi says, "what's wrong with mommy?"

"Nothing." He answers, "She's just had a very bad day obviously. But she's going to be okay. She didn't mean those dirty words."

"I'm worried daddy." Domi replies.

"Hey," he responds and smiles, "don't worry. Mommy's going to be alright. Why don't you run upstairs and wait for daddy to help you get ready for bed."

"Ok." She replies and kisses him on the cheek.

Domi quickly scurries upstairs. Michael turns around and slowly approaches Raylene. She stays on the couch, covering her eyes with her left hand and holding the vodka bottle with her right.

"Care to explain this Ray?" He asks.

"I'm not explaining shit until you cut the fucking lights!" She roars.

He reaches over and pulls the almost empty bottle out of her hand. She lowers her left hand and squints at him, trying to focus.

"Give that back!" She demands.

He takes a few steps back and leans against a wall.

"Give me the damn bottle!" She insists.

"Come get it." He calmly answers. "If you can walk over here, retrieve the bottle, walk back to the couch, sit back down, and take another swig, I'll cut the lights and leave you alone."

Raylene puts her hands on the couch and braces her self. Slowly, she gets up from the couch and faces Michael. She takes a few small steps across the marble floor, and then tumbles face first on it. Pushing herself off the ground, she feel queasy and the room spins faster. She gets back to her feet and promptly falls again. She stays on the ground and cries loudly. Michael sits the bottle down, kneels next to her and gently cradles his fiancée. He wraps her in a firm embrace as she cries into his chest. Minutes elapse and Raylene falls silent, sound asleep in Michael's arms. He scoops her up and carries her to the master bedroom. He lays her on the bed, removes her shoes and pants, and pulls the comforter over her body. He kisses her forehead and leaves her to her slumber.

Michael makes his way across the hall to Dominique's bedroom. He sees his daughter sitting at her desk, doodling in her coloring book and crying. He kneels beside her and squeezes her tightly. She returns the hug.

"Is mommy okay?" She asks.

"Mommy's a little sick right now." He answers. "But I put her to bed and she's sleeping. She'll be okay, I promise."

"I prayed for her daddy." She says.

"That's good." He replies. "That'll help her. You know what'll help you?"

"What?" She asks.

"A nice warm bath." He says.

He takes his daughter by the hand and leads her to the bathroom. He gets her a fresh towel, clean underwear, and her pajamas from a dresser drawer. He turns on the warm water and helps her undress. When the water is high enough, he scoops her up and gives her a tummy kiss before placing her in the tub. He gives her a couple of her favorite tub toys and scoops up her dirty clothes.

"You get good and clean." He says. "I'll be back in a little bit to check on you."

He waits until she begins to play with her toys before he leaves. He carries her dirty clothes to the laundry room and deposits them in a hamper. He jams his right hand into his pocket and heads to his downstairs office. In the office, he closes his door and turns on his computer. After it boots up, he clicks into a directory folder and views the images inside. After flipping through the first few photos, he reaches into his pocket and withdraws a piece of fabric. It is balled in his hand, pink with small strawberries imprinted all over it. He holds it to his nose and inhales deeply. Using his other hand, he unzips his pants, withdraws his phallus and begins to masturbate. He takes the fabric and unravels it. It is a pair of little girl panties, Dominique's worn underwear. He wraps it around his member and continues to masturbate while looking at the photos on his computer. After 20 minutes of viewing and masturbating, he ejaculates into the underwear. He regains his composure, turns off his P.C., and heads back upstairs. He puts the underwear in the washer, along with Domi's other dirty clothes and begins a wash cycle. He then goes back to the bathroom. Domi is out of the tub and drying herself off. Michael places his hands on the towel and helps his daughter dry. He dresses her for bed, takes her to her bedroom, and tucks her in for the night. He kisses her forehead, says goodnight, and leaves her room, closing the door behind him. In the hallway, he wipes the sweat from his brow and goes to the master bedroom.

Tuesday morning at the agency finds Isabella De Oro sitting in wait inside of Raylene's office. After yesterday's shoot, she was taken home and watched by Raylene's bodyguard Ben. He made sure that she went home and slept off the effects of the cocaine after the photo shoot. The shoot went very well, and now she waits to here if she landed the contract with the men's magazine. She wants to be in the office with Raylene when the phone call came in, but the time is 9:00a.m., and Raylene is three hours late. This is not like her and Izzy grows concerned. The door to the office opens and Izzy whips her head around.

"Ray?" She calls out.

"WRONG!" Willow shouts. "Try again bitch."

"Is Ray here yet?" Izzy asks.

"Is Ray here yet?" Willow repeats. "Are you shitting me? After everything that happened yesterday? Fuck no she's not her yet and probably won't come in at all."

"What are you talking about?" Izzy asks. "What happened yesterday?"

Willow almost chokes on her surprise.

"WHAT?" She shouts. "You didn't hear?"

"Hear what?" Izzy demands.

"Raylene has a daughter!" Willow answers.

"D'uh." Izzy replies. "I know. She's five years old and named Domini…"

"No, no, no." Willow interrupts. "Not Domi. Another daughter. The bitch had a kid 20 years ago!"

"Are you serious?" Izzy asks in surprise.

"Yeah." Willow answers. "She came in yesterday for a screening under a fake name. She runs into Raylene on the set, and the shit hits the fan."

"Is she visiting from college or something like that?" Izzy asks.

"Nuh uh." Willow responds. "Ray ditched her seven years ago to live with her grandmother. They haven't seen or talked to each other since until yesterday."

"Oh my God." Izzy utters. "How's she handling it?"

"Oh, she fucking flipped!" Willow answers. "Ray ran off the set in tears screaming no, no, no, and her daughter left the agency the same way. Arpi and I visited Ray in her office afterwards, and she blamed us, accusing us of setting the whole thing up."

"That's so unbelievable." Izzy remarks.

Hera walks into the office.

"Do you guys think mom will mention her illegitimate daughter tonight?" She asks.

"You knew too?" Izzy asks.

"Yeah." Hera responds. "I saw the encounter on the set during Suki's shoot. Arpi filled me in afterwards. I left you a voicemail, didn't you get it?"

Izzy pulled out her cell phone and looks at the dead screen.

"It's dead again!" Izzy exclaims.

"You need to stop buying that cheap Chinese shit." Willow replies.

"We should do something for her tonight." Hera says. "She's been so great to us, we should help take her mind off of it, just until she is ready to comes to grips with it."

"What do you say Willow?" Izzy asks.

"Well Arpi and I are cooking something up," Willow answers, "but it's a surprise."

"Tell us." Izzy pleas.

"Yes tell us." Hera follows.

"Fuck no!" Willow shouts. "I ain't telling you bitches shit."

"You know," Hera says, "you are just so rude at times!"

"Thank you!" Willow replies.

Willow gets up from her seat and leaves the office. Hera and Isabella soon follow.

Ten o'clock in the morning, and Raylene finally stirs from her slumber. She tries to open her eyes, but the morning light sends a piercing pain through her head. She winces, and that slight movement sends a powerful tremor through her brain. Her head pulses, the palms of her hands and feet are numb, her whole body aches, and her mouth taste like pasty vomit. She fights the pain to bring her hand to her head. She touches her pillow and feels a cold, chunky wetness. It smells of Vodka and nachos and makes her nauseous.

She forces her eyes open and surveys the room. Her hangover blurs her vision and destroys her depth perception. Relying on muscle memory, she very slowly heads to her bathroom. With every tiny step, her vision clears slightly. In her bathroom, she splashes cold water on her face and rinses her mouth with mouthwash. She looks at her ravaged visage in the mirror. Her eyes are bloodshot, her wrinkles are deep, and yesterday's makeup is spread everywhere. She takes four painkillers and slowly creeps downstairs.

Reaching the ground floor, she finds a note in the kitchen from Michael.

Hey Gorgeous.

I took Dominique to school this morning and will pick her up. I called your office and they know not to expect you today. Please rest easy. Don't forget, you invited your daughters to the house for dinner tonight. Call me and let me know what to pick up.

Me and Domi Love you
Michael.

"Oh fuck." She mutters to herself.

The events from yesterday flashed in her mind.

"Invited my daughters to dinner." She mutters to herself. "Not all my daughters."

Natalie's morning has been a blur. She slept until almost noon and rummaged through her clothes, trying to find something nice to wear. She cannot believe she is excited about going to her mother's house, despite the events of yesterday. She has a feeling that tonight will be more of the same, but she has to try. If she can get in her mother's good graces, she can have a new beginning, and possibly, a better life.

Later in the afternoon, Arpi and Willow head to the parking garage. Once they pickup the car, they can head out to get Natalie before making their way to Raylene's house.

"You really think Ray is gonna go for this?" Willow asks.

"What do you mean?" Arpi replies.

"I mean us," Willow answers, "forcing her to reconcile with her daughter."

"I'm sure she will be reluctant," Arpi responds, "but this is for her own good. She'll realize that. Besides, how would you feel if you were split from your mother for seven years?"

"I'd love it.' Willow exclaims. "My mom's a whore and a crackhead. Why else do you think I bailed out the house last year?"

"Ok," Arpi replies, "bad example. But still, Ray will thank us after it's all said and done."

They arrive at the car.

"Alright then." Willow says. "Let's go get the heifer."

Evening falls, and Raylene has finally recovered from her hangover. She has arranged her living and dining rooms for her guest. She has looked forward to this evening since last week, but now she feels trepidation. She knew the girls were going to ask her about Natalie, and she did not feel like talking about her. She hoped to intercept each of the girls and asks them not to mention it, especially not around Michael. She did not have any idea as to how he would react. The time is 6:52 p.m. and her guest would so be arriving.

A knock on the door gets Raylene's attention. She opens the door and is greeted by Hera and Isabella. She hugs the girls and welcomes them in. She pours them a glass of wine and wants to start a friendly conversation to relax her mind. She does not get that chance.

"Is it true?" Izzy asks. "Do you really have another daughter?"

Raylene sighs; so much for her relaxing evening.

"I don't want to talk about it." She answers sharply.

"So it is true!" Izzy exclaims.

"I said I don't want to talk about it." Raylene reiterates.

"Mom," Hera cuts in, "you can tell us. You know we won't judge you."

"I wouldn't care if you did." Raylene states. "This is a closed matter."

"What if she goes public?" Izzy cuts in.

Raylene is silent in response and hangs her head down.

"If that happens," Izzy continues, "it could be a stain on your reputation, and the agency. We just want to help in anyway we can."

Raylene could not afford any bad press. Her image is still tarnished in Europe, and she plans to expand there within a few years. If Natalie did go public, she would be seen as a horrible mother and would have difficultly landing new models.

"I'll talk," She begins, "if you promise me one thing."

"Anything." Hera responds. "Just name it."

"Don't you dare mention any of this to Michael or Domi." Raylene says. "If they need to know, I'll tell them."

"Deal." The girls say simultaneously.

Raylene takes a deep breath.

"I wasn't ready for children," She began, "and the pregnancy wasn't planned. I tried to be a good mother, but I was terrible at it. She was just so non-conforming to what I expected. When she was 12, I took her to live with my mother and I moved to L.A. She was supposed to live there and have her life; I never dreamed she would track me down."

"Why don't you just tell her," Hera replies, "that you wanted her to have a better life? That's why you left. I'm sure she'll understand."

"And what if she goes public with that information?" Raylene shoots back. "That would be just as damning. Trust me, it's just better for me to leave it alone. Hopefully she gets the message and goes back to Oregon."

"Don't you think that's a little cruel?" Izzy asks.

"Crueler than what?" Raylene fires back. "The truth, that she was a mistake, an accident from me taking desperate action to get a contract? That she was never meant to be born, and I would have gotten an abortion had I not been concerned about my modeling career? Tell her that she was a curse, not a gift? You tell me Izzy, which action would be crueler to you?"

Izzy cannot respond.

"Anytime you have to pick your poison," Raylene continues, "it's never easy. I've made my choice and that is it. I'm not proud of it, but it's the only choice I can make."

Neither Hera nor Izzy can respond. They silently resign themselves to the fact that Raylene is firm in her decision. They hear a car pull into the driveway.

"Now that you girls have heard me out," she concludes, "can I trust you to keep your end of the bargain and not utter a word of this to Michael or my youngest daughter?"

They girls remain silent and nod their heads in agreement.

"Thank you." Raylene says quietly.

The opening front door gains everyone's attention. Michael walks in with Dominique close in tow. Once again, Michael had to take the precious child to the studio and they arrived a few minutes late. He carries bag of food he picked up from Raylene favorite steakhouse.

"Auntie Hera!" Dominique yells."

She runs to Hera and gives her a big hug. Hera smiles and returns the embrace.

"Hey sweetie." She says. "I've missed you so much!"

"I missed you too." Domi replies and breaks the hug.

She heads over to Isabella.

"Hi Izzy!" She says and gives Isabella a hug.

"Hey angel." Izzy replies. "You've been a good girl?"

"The bestest!" Domi answers.

Michael walks over and exchanges pleasantries with the women, and gives his fiancée a kiss. He then walks over to the dining room table and sets it up for dinner. The females resume their conversation, with no further mention of Natalie. Dominique talked about what she is learning at school and the girls hang on her every word. When the table is set, Michael calls everyone over so they can begin.

"We can't start yet." Raylene protests. "Not without Willow and Arpi."

"They called me ahead of time." Michael responds. "They said they had to finish something up and would be here about a half-hour late."

"Well it would be rude to start without them." Raylene insists. "We will wait."

"But Mommy," Dominique cut in, "I'm hungry."

"Young lady," Raylene shots back, "you do as you're…"

DING DONG.

The doorbell rings.

"You see?" Raylene piques happily. "That didn't take long."

"I'll get it." Michael says to Raylene. "You sit down."

Raylene takes a seat at the table and smiles at her girls. Michael gets to the front door and opens it. He looks out and sees Arpi and Willow, as he expected, and a third young lady he had never met before. She is slightly taller than average height, long blond hair, creamy tan skin, and supple young body.

"Good evening ladies." Michael exclaims.

Arpi and Willow return the greeting, but do so timidly. The blond does not speak, and stares away nervously.

"You two brought a friend?" He asks. "Well the more, the merrier, c'mon in."

He steps aside so the girls can enter the house. He leads them from the entry and into the dining room. The other ladies are happily talking amongst themselves, and no one initially notices the three girls enter.

"They have arrived," Michael says, "and they've brought a friend."

Raylene and the other girls look up and the room falls silent. They lock stares with Willow, Arpi, and the third female. Isabella looks around nervously and wonders what just happened. Dominique continues to drink her lemonade and fight her hunger. Hera diverts her gazes from the three girls over to Raylene; who stares with building anger.

Natalie has never felt so nervous in her life. As she stands in the middle of her mother's house, she can feel the multiple stares tear through her. She looks around and sees the eyes of everyone in the room, and stops at Raylene. Once again, the two were locked in a stare down. Michael is confused.

"Did I miss something earlier?" He asks.

Raylene stands up from the table, and stares at Arpi.

"What is the meaning of this?" She bellows. "Bringing her to my home, how could you?"

"This is about doing what is best for you!" Arpi answers sharply. "What's best for both of you!"

"How dare you decide what is best for me?" Raylene demands. "I'm not ready for all this. What makes you think I can handle this right now?"

"I dunno." Willow interrupts. "Maybe the fact you gave birth to her."

Michael chokes up on his wine at Willow's statement and Dominique gasps.

"WHAT?" Izzy shouts. "She's the daughter?'

"Izzy!" Hera shoots back before whispering. "You weren't supposed to say anything in front of Domi."

Isabella takes a quick glance at Dominique and realizes her folly.

"Oh shi…crap.!" She says.

"What was that?" Michael asks after he is able to breathe again. "Gave birth to her?"

Raylene hangs her head shamefully, but doesn't answer.

"It's true!" Natalie says. "My name is Natalie Cordova, and Raylene is my mother. Seven years ago, you left me in Oregon when you came out here, and I never heard from you again."

Michael slowly walks over to Raylene.

"Is it true Ray?" He asks. "She's your daughter?"

"I can't do this right now." She quietly answers. "Please make her leave."

"Answer my question." He insists. "Is she you daughter?"

Raylene begins to weep, but does not answer; only looks away. Michael looks over to Arpi and Natalie.

"Can you prove this?" He asks. "Or is this some kind of sick joke?"

"It's true." Raylene mutters. Michael looks back at her.

"What was that?" he asks.

"It's true." Raylene whispers. "She is my daughter."

Michael is stunned and does not know how to react. He quickly looks over at Natalie, but does not know what to say. Arpi steps in a leans close to Raylene.

"You have to do what's right Ray." She says quietly. "Talk to her. Come to some sort of resolution."

Arpi looks over at Michael.

"Domi doesn't need to see mommy like this." She says and nods toward the girl.

"Oh." Michael exclaims. "Right."

He breaks away and goes over to Dominique.

"Let's go to the game room pumpkin," he says, "so mommy and the girl can talk."

He scoops up his daughter into his arms.

"That's a good idea." Arpi says. "Let's all go to the game room and leave them alone."

The guests start to leave the room.

"But I want to see this." Izzy protests.

Willow walks up and pops Isabella in the back of the head.

"You heard the man." She says. "To the game room. Mueva su asno usted hembra."

"¡Amartille a la puta que chupa!" Izzy shouts.

"¡Asno que bebe ruidosamente pedo de gatito!" Willow shoots back.

Willow, Arpi, Michael, Hera, Isabella, and Dominique leave the dining room and head to the game room, leaving Natalie and Raylene alone. Natalie keeps her stare on her mother, while Raylene looks down at the carpet. She continues to cry, unable to cope with the situation, and not sure what to say.

"You can't runaway this time." Natalie begins. "Please, face me."

Slowly, Raylene raises her gaze from the floor and moves up Natalie's body. She begins at her daughter's feet and moves up her legs. Each inch she goes higher, her emotions make it more difficult to continue. Reaching her mid-drift, Raylene has to wipe her eyes and stop for a second. Continuing up, she finally stares Natalie in the face. The girl's deep blue eyes matched her own, along with the sandy blond hair. The radiant skin and high cheekbones were along the same lines as her. Looking at Natalie was like staring into a painful past, a past that had finally caught up to her.

"Why are you here?" Raylene asks quietly.

"I don't know why I came," Natalie answers, "but it just seemed like the right thing to do."

"Right for whom?" Raylene asks.

"Right for me." Natalie answers. "I couldn't stay there anymore, not with that woman. I just wanted to be with my mother, and try to have a normal life."

"I tried to give you a normal life." Raylene replies. "You resisted. You wanted to be a kid."

"I was a kid!" Natalie shoots back. "I was a kid, and wanted to live a kid life! I wanted to make friends and play with them. I wanted to get dirty, and maybe even play a sport and break a bone, and have a cast for my friends to sign. What was wrong with that?"

"That wasn't my plan for you." Raylene responds.

"Your plan for me?" Natalie asks, tears welling in her eyes. "You never even consulted me! I was forced to live a lifestyle I hated. You forced me to standby, while you lived vicariously through me! I wanted to live my life, not yours."

"And do what with that life?" Raylene roars. "Be ordinary, blend in, be just another piss-ant in the ever flushing toilet of life? Had I not tried to shape you, you might have become a high school slut, pregnant before your 15th birthday."

"At least, it would have been my choice." Natalie replies.

"Your choices were always shit!" Raylene exclaims. "You made poor choices in places you wanted to go, things you wanted to do, and everything else. You just refused to learn."

"How am I supposed to learn," Natalie responds, "if I'm never allowed to make mistakes?"

"You want to make mistakes?" Raylene asks. "Well congratulations, you just made you first one, and it's a doozy!"

"Wrong!" Natalie says. "My first mistake was not telling you how I felt about how you raised me. That's a mistake I plan to fix, right here, right now."

"You have no right…" Raylene begins.

"I HAVE EVEY RIGHT!" Natalie screams. "You kept me quiet at every turn in life, and then got rid of me when it was convenient for you. I have earned the right to stand here and vent. SO YOU WILL SHUT THE FUCK UP AND LISTEN TO EVERY GODDAMN WORD I HAVE TO SAY!"

Raylene is taken aback by her daughter's sudden anger, and falls back into a chair. Startled, she keeps an attentive stare on her daughter. Natalie clears her throat and pulls her hair back.

"I hated it." Natalie begins tearfully. "I had no freedom to talk to you, to let you know how I felt about things. I was polarized in school, and all the kids hated me. I had no friends, and no one to make me feel better, not even you. You never held me, consoled me when I cam home in tears, and crying. I was abused in school, and emotionally tortured everyday. But instead of making me feel loved, you told me it was my fault and that I deserved everything that was happening to me. My mother left me alone in the cold cruel world."

Raylene cannot respond, only cry.

"But I never stopped loving you." Natalie continued. "I made myself believe, that you knew what was best for me. I wanted to be just like you, but I did not know how, and you would not teach me. I never felt any love in return."

Natalie can barely control her emotions and the tears begin to flow. She wipes them away, but they are quickly replaced by new one. With this moment of silence, Raylene has a chance to respond.

"What do you what from me?" She asks.

"Why couldn't you just love me mom?" Natalie cries. "What did I do, to make you hate me? Why did you abandon me?"

"Oh Natalie." Raylene answers. "Of course I loved you. You were my daughter. I raised you as best I could, but I couldn't do it anymore. I needed a clean start, and I couldn't provide a good life for you anymore. I had a great life with your grandmother, and I figure she could give you a life I never could."

Natalie remains silent, so Raylene take advantage.

"It was utterly," she continues, "the hardest decision I have ever made in my life. To this day I would wonder what could have been had I kept you with me. But I was young and scared then, and not ready to deal with a reluctant child."

Natalie's tears increase.

"I cried myself to sleep every night for a year since that day." She goes on. "I would cry, and speak your name, hoping it would get easier. But it never did."

"Why didn't you send for me?" Natalie asks.

"Part of me wanted to, in the worst way." Raylene answers. "But my life had to continue, and so did yours. Yes, it was painful, but I made my choice, and I don't regret it. I left you to your life, and I was hoping you would leave me to mine."

"So even today," Natalie replies, "you want nothing to do with me. You despise me still."

"I don't despise you Natalie," Raylene responds, her voice hardening, "but I am annoyed at this interruption at what was once a peaceful existence."

Raylene turns her head to avoid looking at the girl. Natalie can hear the anger in her mother's voice and stops crying. She had learned in college to never back down from any challenge, and she would not stop now. She steps up to Raylene and gets in her face.

"Look me in the eye mom." She says. "Look me in the eye, and tell me you cannot stand me. Tell me you hate me, and you want me gone. If you can do that, I'll go, and bother you no more."

Raylene turns her head slowly to face Natalie. Both of their faces are wet and red from this emotional confrontation. Raylene stares at her daughter, but cannot speak. She cannot bear to tell her that she wishes she had never shown up. Deep down, she wishes she was never born. Natalie takes her silence as reluctance.

"You can't, can you?" She asks. "There's something inside of you, that wants me around; and until you accept me as part of yourself, I'm sticking around. Unlike what you did to me, I'm not giving up on you."

With that statement, Natalie heads for the front door, exits the house, and slams the door hard. Raylene lowers her head and cries hard.

Inside the game room, Michael starts an inquisition into the new turn of events.

"Talk to me Arpi." He says. "What's going on here?"

"Ray had a kid 19 years ago." Arpi answers. "She left Natalie with her grandmother seven years ago and came out here."

"Do you even know how ludicrous that sounds?" He asks. "Why would she have not told me?"

"She was ashamed." Arpi answers. "She wanted to forget about her."

"Before you got here," Hera cuts in, "she said Natalie was a mistake and she should have aborted her."

"What?" He shoots back. "You knew about this? How many of you guys knew about this girl?"

"I found out his morning from Hera." Izzy answers.

"She came to the agency yesterday under a fake name." Willow says. "Caught us all off guard."

"Daddy," Domi says, "do I have a big sister?"

Michael is at a loss for words. The truth is yes, that Domi now has a big sister, but if Raylene will not accept her, then what should he tell his daughter. He thinks fast.

"I don't know." He answers. "That's up to Mommy."

"I hope so!" Domi replies. "I've always wanted a big sister."

"I HAVE EVEY RIGHT!" They hear Natalie scream.

"Sounds like fun out there." Willow remarks.

"Maybe I should be out there." Michael says.

Arpi blocks his path.

"No." She insists. "Raylene has to face her daughter, and do this alone."

"She did want to hide it from you." Izzy cuts in.

"Raylene hides nothing from me." He replies.

"She asked us not to say anything around you," Hera interrupts, "or Domi."

Michael looks resigned and feels helpless. He wants to support Ray, but is hurt by her desire to hide what is going on. Before he can formulate his next thought, he hears the front door slam. The slam is so hard that it shakes the walls. Michael and the girls race out the game room and find Raylene standing by herself in the middle of the dining room crying. Michael walks over to his fiancée and wraps his arms around her, trying to comfort her. Dominique, Hera, and Isabella join him. Arpi and Willow sneak out the front door.

Natalie stands outside and leans on Arpi's car. She hangs her head, but does not cry. Her mother doesn't want her around, but cannot say it to her face. She takes that as a concession, and a reason to keep trying. After a minute of silent contemplation, she looks up and sees Willow and Arpi headed over to her.

"How'd it go?" Arpi asks.

"Not like I wanted," Natalie begins, "but better than I imagined. She may want me gone, but she can't come out and say it. Part of her wants me around."

"Awesome!" Willow exclaims. "That's fucking great."

"Yeah, it's a start." Natalie replies. "I think I'll stick around, and keep fighting for her."

While Willow and Natalie make idle chatter about what happened in the house, Arpi hangs her head and curses to herself. Her plan had not worked. Raylene did not further the rejection, and now Natalie has hope. If Raylene's shield cracks, then Arpi could find herself replaced. Arpi has one more trick left, but she has to wait until tomorrow to play it. She looks up at Natalie.

"You need a ride back to the hotel?" She asks.

"That would be great," Natalie says, "but shouldn't you guys stay here?"

"After what we just pulled," Willow begins, "Ray doesn't want us here, and we'll be lucky if we're not fired first thing in the morning."

The three girls laugh at the statement and get in the car. Arpi starts the engine and drives off.

Two hours pass, and the last two girls have left the house. Raylene was put to bed soon after the incident and is resting peacefully. Michael finishes tucking in Domi and kisses her goodnight. He returns to his bedroom and finds his fiancée awake in the bed.

"We need to talk." She says.

"Yes we do." He replies. "But only when you're ready."

"I'm never going to be ready," she says, "so let's just get it over with."

Michael takes a deep breathe.

"When were you going to tell me about Natalie?" He asks.

"I wasn't." She answers. "You were never meant to know."

"Why not?" He asks.

"I thought it was a closed chapter of my life." Raylene answers. "She wasn't supposed to return to me."

"Ray," he says, "I don't know if there are any right words to say about all this. Just know this, whatever you chose to do, I support you one hundred percent, and will stand in your corner."

"Thank you." She replies. "And when I decide what to do, you will know."

"Alright." He says. "Goodnight my sweet."

They exchange their kisses and lay their heads down. Michael falls right asleep. Raylene is sleepless the rest of the night.

Nine o'clock Wednesday morning and Keri is cleaning out her desk at the agency. She accepted an internship with a Miami based marketing firm two weeks ago, and today is her last day. She was reluctant to break the news to anyone but Raylene, so none of the models knew. She tries to be covert in her actions when Willow walks in and sees her.

"Oh my God!" She exclaims. "Are you quitting?"

"I turned in my two weeks notice two weeks ago." Keri says. "I got a job in Miami in marketing. Today is my last day."

"You bitch!" Willow shouts. "When were you gonna fucking tell me?"

"Today," Keri answers, "maybe. I didn't want anyone to cause a scene."

Willow throws her arms around Keri and hugs her.

"I'm gonna miss you K." She says. "Who's gonna put up with my shit now?"

"I'm sure you'll find someone." Keri says as she breaks the hug. "Wait here a second. I gotta run to the can."

Keri grabs her purse and heads to the office door. As she walks out Natalie walks in. Willow sees her and runs to the door.

"Whassup bitch." Willow says, giving her usual greeting.

"Same to you." Natalie replies.

"So how you been?" Willow asks.

"Pretty good." Natalie answers. "I kind of feel like I'm riding some momentum from last night. I know I shouldn't rush anything, but I was hoping she was in right now."

"Obviously," Willow begins, "you have no idea about how badly you fucked her shit up mentally. She had never been late or missed a single day of work ever since I've been here. Since you came around, she missed work yesterday, and is three hours late today, so far."

"I've been told I have that effect on people." Natalie jokes. "So I guess I have no reason to be here."

"You do now." Willow replies. "My girl Keri is leaving us today. Taking a plush job in Miami. So you are going to come with me to take her out and say goodbye."

"But I don't even know her." Natalie protests.

"I don't give a fuck!" Willow responds.

At this moment, Keri re-enters the suite.

"Good news K." Willow says. "Me and my girl Natalie are gonna take you out to say goodbye."

"No can do hun." Keri replies. "My cab is waiting outside, and my flight leaves in four hours."

"But you can't leave so soon." Willow says. "That's so fucked up!"

"Sorry babe," Keri says, "but duty calls."

She walks up to Willow and gives her a final hug and kiss on the cheek.

"I'll miss you Will." She says. "Tell the girls I love them all."

"I'll miss you too," Willow replies, "you fucking cunt."

Keri takes her box of belongings and heads for the door. She gives a friendly wave to Natalie and exits the office. Natalie looks at Willow.

"Can I leave now?" She asks.

"Fuck no!" Willow exclaims. "Now I need some cheering up. Come on."

Willow grabs Natalie by the arm and leads her out of the office. They board the elevator and ride down to the parking garage. They climb into Willow's car and leave the building. Willow never mentions were they are heading, but Natalie doesn't mind. They talk and tell jokes while en route. The drive out to North Hollywood, pull up to a house and park. They get out of the car and walk to the front door. Willow knocks on the door.

"Where are we?" Natalie asks.

"The happiest place on earth." Willow answers. "Or in L.A. at least."

The door opens and a young man emerges. Before he can recognize his guest or say anything to them, Willow jumps on him and wraps her arms and legs around him.

"Ben, my love!" She exclaims.

"Willow." He replies. "What are you doing here? I thought you were booked all afternoon."

"I am," she replies, "but it's early in the morning and I need an A.M. pick me up."

"What kind of pick me up?" He asks and grabs a handful of her backside.

"Slow down asshole," she protests, "we have company."

He looks at the door and sees a blond girl watching them. He quickly composes himself, puts Willow down and stands at attention.

"Ben this is Natalie," Willow begins, "Natalie, this is my boy toy Ben."

"How are you doing?" Ben asks.

"Just fine, thanks." Natalie replies.

"So Ben," Willow cuts back in, "what have you got for me?"

"In regards to what?" He asks.

"Don't play dumb fucker!" Willow yells. "You got some shit or not?"

"Willow," he interjects, "I can't keep doing that. I'll lose my job and get arrested!"

Ben may only by a rookie cop, but he found out about certain perks of his job. When at the station, he has access to the evidence lockup in the narcotics division. His best friend is in charge of that area, and lets him take a little marijuana every now and them, as well as other drugs. The precinct has begun to crackdown of such activities, so his pickings have been very slim as of late. Whatever he can get, he shares with Willow.

"You'll fucking lose me if you don't give me what I need!" Willow shoots back.

"Alright." He concedes. "Alright, come in."

He steps aside and lets the girls inside. After he closes the door, he opens a chest next to his couch. Inside, Natalie can see all sorts of syringes, bottles, pipes, and bongs, along with a large bag of Mary Jane. He lifts the bag of pot, and fishes underneath it. He pulls out a smaller bag containing more marijuana, but the contents are purple.

"This stuff," he begins, "we got off a Russian dude with ties to mob. I think it's imported from the Netherlands."

He tosses the bag to Willow.

"Papers?" She asks.

"Right here." He answers.

He reaches into the chest and gives Willow some paper to roll a joint. They sit together on the couch and Willow rolls them each a joint with the purple weed. As they begin to smoke, Natalie digs through the chest and pulls out a brown bottle and a small vial containing a clear liquid.

"What are these?" Natalie asks.

Ben looks up.

"The bottle is chloroform," He answers. "A small amount of the vapor causes a nice high, but too much will knock you out. That small one is sodium pentobarbital."

"Sodium pentobarbital?" She asks. "What does that do?"

"Don't know what is does to humans." He answers. "We got it from a vet that was selling firearms in the back of his office."

He starts to giggle as the purple bud takes effect. Willow giggles in response.

"This is pet medicine?" Natalie asks.

"Nope." He answers. "It makes Lassie go night-night forever."

Willow laughs hysterically at his remark.

"You're so funny baby." She says. "This shit's making me hot."

She leans in and kisses him hard on the mouth. He grabs her hair and returns the kiss. They make out ferociously. Using the distraction, Natalie puts the chloroform and the smaller bottle in her purse. She also finds a syringe and takes one too. She looks back at the couch and sees Ben taking Willow's top off.

"I'll leave you two alone." Natalie says.

"No." Willow says. "Hold up, I'm coming."

Willow stands off the couch.

"Please no." Ben pleads. "I want you so bad."

"Just think of me while you whack it." Willow replies.

She gets off the couch and walks out the front door. Natalie follows closely behind her. Depressed, Ben sits alone on the couch. Deciding to take her advice, he unzips his pants.

Outside, Willow, leans on Natalie as they stumble towards her car. She hasn't stopped giggling since she walked out the house. She digs in her purse and pulls out her keys. Natalie quickly takes them away from her.

"WTF ho!" Willow shouts.

Natalie reaches over and takes the joint as well. She holds them both up.

"Drive or smoke." She says. "Pick one."

"Drive or smoke." Willow repeats. "Drive or smoke. Drive or smoke. Drive or smoke."

She develops a musical rhythm as she repeats the phrase and starts to giggle again. Natalie places the joint back to Willow's lips and the girl sucks on it hungrily.

"Just tell me where to go." Natalie says.

Willow nods her head in agreement and blows smoke from her nose. Natalie leads the little stoner to the passenger side. She opens the door and sits her down in the car. Once she is in the driver seat, Willow pulls out a brochure and points to it. It is for a tattoo parlor on Melrose Blvd. called 'The Sacred Stain.' Natalie takes the brochure and punches the address into the car's navigation system. After the directions came up, they were on their way.

After only ten minutes of driving, Natalie determined she hated L.A. drivers. She was cut off twice, flipped of once, and had difficulty merging on the freeway. After a 30 minute adventure, they arrived at the shop. Fortunately, Willow's high had begun to rescind.

"Come on bitch." She says and exits the car.

Natalie exits the car, locks it, and follows Willow inside. This shop was very different from her hometown. The shop at home seemed very quiet, clean and professional. The Sacred Stain however, was very loud, crowded, and very rowdy. No less than 30 patrons were inside. Only six were getting tattoos, the rest were just hanging out.

"Willow!" A female voice rings out. "You foxy bitch!"

Whassup Kittyhawk!" Willow shouts back.

Willow runs over to a woman on the far side of the shop. The women hug and begin to chat. As they converse, an older man walks behind Willow and smacks her on the backside. Willow angrily turns around.

"You fuck!" She screams.

She grabs the cordless phone off the nearby countertop and smacks him over the head with it. He falls on the floor bleeding from the head. She doesn't stop. She jumps on top of him, repeated hitting him with the broken phone, deepening the gash on his forehead. His blood coats her hand and seems to drive her on. The other woman pulls Willow off the guy and calls someone else over.

"Bull!" She yells. "Take this fuck to the back and beat his ass!"

A large black man arrives, grabs the older man off the floor and drags him to the back of the shop.

"I'll rip your fucking balls off!" Willow screams as he is taken away.

The other woman looks at Willow.

"Are you okay hun?" She asks.

"Can you believe that asshole?" Willow asks. "Hey Natalie! Get your cute ass over here!"

Natalie walks over to the two women.

"Nat," Willow begins, "this is my home girl Kitty. She owns this place."

Natalie shakes hands with the owner and checks her out. She is in her early thirties with tattoos completely covering her arms, legs, neck, and upper chest. Not a single centimeter of natural skin could be seen, save for her face, with was half covered in butterflies.

"Nice to meet you Kitty." Natalie says.

"Likewise." Kitty replies. "So what can we do for you bitches?"

"I need something fresh. "Willow says. "The back of my neck is boring."

Kitty walks behind Willow and takes a look.

"I'm thinking," she begins, "dragonfly."

"Sweet." Willow replies. "What about you Nat? Where's your next one going?"

"I haven't even though that far out yet." Natalie answers.

"I didn't think you were the inking type." Kitty says.

"Check it out." Natalie responds.

She turns around and lifts the back of her shirt. Kitty checks out the black widow and the victimized bee. She touches the tattoos in her appreciation.

"Nice." She remarks. "How long did that one take?"

"Three hours." Natalie answers. "Did it all in one sitting."

"Tell you what." Kitty says. "You let me add me own touches to it, then I'll do you and Willow on the house."

"Deal." Natalie agrees.

They head to two empty seats and get ready. Kat calls over on of her best artist to tend to Willow while she starts on Natalie. Kitty preps her needle and rubs Natalie's back before beginning.

"Anything you want to incorporate before we begin?" She asks.

"Now that you mention it, yes." Natalie answers.

She grabs a piece of paper and scribbles on it. She gives it to Kitty. Written on the paper are the letters M, M, L, H, A, H, and R, in random places.

"These letters have special meaning to you?" Kitty asks.

"Most definitely." Natalie answers.

"Alright," Kitty says, "here we go."

Kitty begins her work and the procedure last for one hour and 15 minutes. She draws intricate and unique blood splatters around the spider and bee. In the middle of each splatter, is one of the letters Natalie had selected. After the work is completed, Natalie inspects the additions to her art.

"I like it." She says. "Better than I could have imagined."

"Damn straight." Kitty replies. "I aim to please."

She turns Natalie around and treats the artwork with ointment and wraps it. When Kitty is done, they walk over to Willow's chair and wait for her. Willow's dragonfly was just finished and the artist dresses it. Natalie is very impressed with the details. Willow gets up and looks at her comrades.

"How's it look?" She asks.

"It's beautiful." Natalie answers. "It fits you perfectly."

"Kitty knows her stuff." Willow replies.

"Yes I do." Kitty says.

She reaches into her pocket and pulls out a business card. She hands it to Natalie.

"If you're going to be in town for a while," she begins, "you're welcome back anytime. A friend of Willow's is a friend of mine. Any ink you want is on the house."

"Thanks Kitty." Natalie replies and gives Kitty a hug.

"Let's go Nat." Willow says. "I have a shoot I gotta prep for."

The girls exchange their goodbye with Kitty and leave the shop. Willow's high has completely subsided and she resumes driving. After a stop at a drive-thru burger joint, they head back to the agency. They arrive and head up to the main office. They walk to the back and Willow begins prep for her shoot.

Arpi storms into the agency at 3:00pm. She skips the counter, does not acknowledge anyone she passes and heads right towards Raylene's office. Raylene is on the phone trying to get a hold of someone. The phone rings a few times before a machine answers. She leaves a message.

"Rebecca," She says, "this is the seventh time today I have called you. Natalie is here, and you were supposed to keep her there. Call me back immediately. Bye."

As she hangs up the phone Arpi walks in.

"I don't care to see you right now." Raylene says.

"I have to know Mom." Arpi says. "This girl can kill everything we have worked to build, and I need to know if you are going to let that happen."

"What in God's name are you talking about?" Raylene asks.

"She's your daughter." Arpi says. "She carries your name, but that's it. She has no experience, she is emotionally disturbed, she forces her will onto other people, and she wants to be a model with our agency? What happens when she meets with a prospective client? She won't know what to do and blow the whole thing. How is that going to look on you?"

"If you are so concerned," Raylene begins, "then why have you and Willow been trying to broker reconciliation?"

"I haven't mom." Arpi answers. "Look, I'm sorry for my behavior, but I know you hate being backed into a corner and you respond in kind. I thought by constantly bringing her to you, you would lay down the law and get rid of her. But she still thinks there's hope for her."

"Arpi." Raylene responds. "She thinks that because I can't tell her that I hate her. I can't hate her, she's my daughter, but I can say honestly, that I don't love her. There is no chance for her here. Please understand that it's just very difficult to tell her right now, because this situation was so unexpected."

"What can't you tell her?" Arpi asks tearfully.

"That I wish she was never born." Raylene says. "She was the mistake that ruined my life at the time. I wish I could have been a better mother, but the past is the past, and I don't want to patch a broken relationship."

She walks up to Arpi and put her hands on her shoulders.

"I always did want a daughter." She continues. "A daughter to continue my legacy, to carry herself in a way that a prosperous woman should. I found that daughter in you Arpi. I don't need a blood relation to have everything I need. As far as I am concerned, you are my true daughter, not Natalie, and nothing is going to ever change that."

Arpi take a second to comprehend her words. They make her feel better, and she is more at ease than ever before.

"I'll help you Mom." She replies. "I'll help you get rid of her. What ever you need just let me know."

"That's my girl." Raylene says.

She pulls Arpi into a tight embrace. They remain that way for a while in silent contemplation. Outside the office door, Natalie has heard every word of the conversation. Her heart pounds in her chest and tears rush down her face. Her face is beet red and her skin is flush.

No chance!

Natalie accepts reality. She has no chance to reconnect with her mother. She was prepared for that. What she was not prepared for, was to hear that she was a mistake. That statement ripped through her like a dull, rusty knife.

No love!

Natalie bows her head and pulls her hair. She wants to scream, but the sound and air eludes her.

The choice is made!

She feels her sadness turn to anger.

Correct the mistake!

Her anger turns to rage.

Kill her!

Her rage turns to hate.

Kill them all!

She lets it consume her.

Natalie takes a deep cleansing breath, dries her eyes, puts a smile on her face, and walks into Raylene's office. Arpi and Raylene break their embrace, startled at the emergence of the lost daughter.

"Good afternoon." She says brightly. "How is everyone doing?"

"Natalie!" Arpi yelps. "We just...um..."

"You know," Natalie interrupts, "I did a shitload of thinking and drinking last night. Thinking about the past, and what's been going on these past couple of days, and I've come to realize that this is all wrong. Mom, or Ray, we have no future together."

"What?" Raylene asks in disbelief.

"You've always been set in your ways." Natalie continues. "You sent to me to Nana's for a reason. Whatever that reason is, you're standing by it, and I now see, there is no moving you. I was wrong to expect anything else."

"So," Raylene replies timidly, "what happens from here? Are you leaving?"

"No." Natalie answers. "Not quite. I think I've discovered a way for us both to move on, seeing as how I have leverage over you."

"What are you talking about?" Raylene demands. "What leverage?"

"I'm not an idiot Ray." Natalie answers. "If word of these past few days goes public, it would be a P.R. nightmare. Good luck having parents trust you with your daughters."

"So that's your game." Raylene replies. "Extortion? Blackmail? Apri, get my checkbook."

"Those are such nasty words." Natalie says while taking a seat. "But let us agree that my silence does have a price."

Raylene is not an idiot either. She knows what Natalie says is true, and could prove to be a weight on her business. If she denied the allegation, Natalie's blood could prove her claim. Then she could face a lawsuit. She would be wise to make this issue just go away so she can return to a normal life.

"How much for your silence?" Raylene concedes.

How much?" Natalie asks. "You think I want money? Expand your horizons chica. I don't want your money."

"Then want do you want?" Raylene asks.

"I want a job." Natalie answers.

"What?" Raylene stammers. "A job? You want to model for me?"

"Oh hell no!" Natalie replies. "I don't want to model. You see, I like L.A., and think I want to stay here. But I can't do that without a job now can I? I know your receptionist's last day was today, and you have no one to man the phone. I want that job."

"Why would you want to be a receptionist?" Arpi asks.

"It's only temporary." Natalie responds. "Just until I find something else, away from all this. I'll use the money to rent an apartment, and go back to school. As soon as I secure another job, I'll leave, and you guys will never hear from me again."

"What guarantees do I have," Raylene shoots in, "that you'll honor your word and keep you silence?"

"You don't." Natalie answers. "But at least this way, you have a chance. The ball is in your court."

Raylene is pinned. If she has any chance of burying this ordeal, she has to take Natalie's offer. She clears her mind, then turns to Arpi.

"Arpi." She says. "Please give Miss Cordova an employment application and new hire agreement."

"Thank you Miss Cordova." Natalie says. "You won't regret this."

"I'd better not." Raylene replied.

Willow finishes her photo session and changes back into street clothes. In the changing room, she runs into Hera and Izzy.

"Whassup bitches." She exclaims.

"I wouldn't be too happy if I was you." Hera remarks.

"Why not?" Willow asks.

"Ray is pissed at you and Arpi." Izzy answers. "She came in today fuming. Why would you bring that girl to her house?"

"Hey," Willow defends, "I'm not the one here alienating my fucking kid. This is what's best for Ray."

"Since when do you know what's best for anyone?" Izzy asks. "You can't even take care of yourself."

"Excuse me," Willow yells, "but since when do I take self-help lessons from a crack whore?"

Izzy is stunned silent.

"What?" Hera blurts.

"I know all about you bitch." Willow goes on. "You show all the symptoms. You fidget when you're alone and nervous, you have rolled twenties in your makeup drawer, you leave white powder dust in your private dressing rooms, and let's not forget the gram of coke Arpi and I found in your damn purse. SO DON'T GIVE ME THAT FUCKING HOLIER THAN THOU ART BULLSHIT!!!!"

Izzy reacts and slaps Willow, knocking her to the ground.

"FUCK YOU!" She screams and runs out the dressing room in tears.

Hera gets out of her seat and chases her. Willow gets off the ground and takes a seat at the makeup desk. She pounds her fist, curses herself, and sulks.

"Fuck." She mutters.

Natalie is at the front desk, rummaging through the many things at her new workstation. She knows her employment will be rough, but she needs to hang around. She needs time to find weaknesses. She has an in-route to the inner workings of the agency through Willow and she plans to exploit it. She might as well begin now. She heads to the back to find her. She walks to the door she believes to be Willow's dressing room and opens it.

"Hey Will I...," She begins but stops.

Inside the dressing room is a crying Izzy. She is leaning over her vanity, face down, with her nose pointing at a small pile of white powder, snorting it. Natalie quickly turns and heads back into the hallway.

Natalie remembers that girl from the party the previous night. She sat at the table next to Raylene, and got smacked in the back of her head by Willow. If she was at the house, then she is close to Raylene, and has an obvious weakness; an addiction to cocaine.

Natalie lowers her head and chuckles to herself. She had just found her first opening.

That night, Raylene arrives home and finds Michael and Domi waiting for her. She gets a big hug and a kiss from her daughter and sends her upstairs so she can talk to Daddy. Domi goes to her bedroom.

"So," Michael begins, "how'd the day go."

"Just fine." Raylene answers. "Michael, I'm sorry for hiding Natalie from you, but it was a shameful chapter in my past that I didn't care to re-live."

"I forgive you." He says. "So what happens next?"

"Nothing." She answers. "She stopped by today, and said she would no longer pursue it. That we can go back to our normal lives. She will not acknowledge me as her mother, and I in turn will not have her forced into my life, our life."

"But that's not right." He protests. "How can you write-off your daughter?"

"It's not a write-off." Raylene answers. "It's a mutual understanding. I'm not dismissing my daughter; I'm protecting our daughter from a stressful and potentially harmful situation."

"But don't you think she'll want to meet her sister?" He asks.

"She needs to be a child." Raylene replies. "We'll let her live her life. When she's older, if she wishes to meet Natalie, then she can." She wraps her arms around him and draws him close.

"You promised me," she continues, "to support me in whatever decision I made. Please say you'll keep your promise."

He looks her in the eyes and lightly kisses her lips.

"I promise." He says.

"Good." She replies. "I'm going to jump in the shower. Care to join me?"

"I'd love to," he begins, "but I have to review production agreements right now."

"That's too bad," She says, "because I am very horny right now."

"Just save some of that fire for me tonight." He replies and kisses her.

As Raylene heads upstairs, Michael heads to his private office. Once inside, he closes and locks the door. He turns on his computer and returns to his favorite file folder. He mutes the sound and plays a video clip. While watching he begins to sweat profusely. He unzips his pants, pulls out his member, and begins to masturbate. The video clip continues and he picks up his pace. Using his free hand, he reaches into his pocket and pulls out a pair of panties. They are white and pink cotton panties he pulled from Domi's clothes hamper. He holds the material to his nose and inhales deeply. His chest tightens and his pulse quickens. He wraps the underwear around his penis and climaxes furiously.

He regains his composure after a minute and looks at his screen. The clip is almost complete. He pauses the screen and stares at it.

"That's a good little girl." He utters under his breathe.

He straightens his clothes, turns off his computer, and heads upstairs. After kissing his daughter goodnight, he heads to his bathroom. Once inside, he strips naked and joins his woman in the shower.

Natalie arrives at her new job bright and early Thursday morning. She tests the door to the suite and is surprised to find it open. After walking in, she finds Arpi at the desk, waiting for her.

"Good morning Natalie." Arpi greets.

"Good morning boss." Natalie replies.

A small chuckle escapes Arpi.

"Are you ready to begin?" She asks.

"Lead the way." Natalie responds.

Arpi gives Natalie a set of office keys, and shows her how to work the computer system for the office. Not only is Natalie a receptionist, she is also the administrative assistant. She is given access to all office systems pertaining to finance, booking, appointment, contract modification, and everybody's e-mail boxes. Arpi takes her around the office and shows her which keys open which doors. All areas are open to her. The job expectations include client correspondence, filing, billing, book keeping, answering the phones, setting up appointments, and other task that Raylene assigns. Natalie takes notes and plays the role of the eager trainee.

"Are you sure you want to do this?" Arpi asks. "I mean, I thought you wanted a meaningful relationship with Ray."

"Sometimes," Natalie begins, "you just have to take what you can get. I figure this is all part of moving on."

"Very well." Arpi responds. "Okay, so Raylene should be here in about an hour. She expects a hot cup of coffee to be waiting for her on her desk as well as a summary of yesterday's expense report. I'll be back at about 12:30pm or so."

"Ok." Natalie replies. "See you then."

Natalie reaches out and gives Arpi a big hug. Arpi is caught off-guard, but decides to return the gesture.

"Alright." She says. "See you later." Arpi leaves.

Fucking bitch!

Natalie's smile quickly disappears. She feels her headache grow and sits at her desk. The feeling of dread spreads through her. She knows what she came to do, but in order to fly under the radar, she would have to engage in endless busy work. Before she attended to her duties, she logged on to the e-mail system. She knows that nothing will be in her inbox yet, so she checks on everyone else. Nothing of interest is in Willow's box, but did find something in Raylene's. A woman named Georgia Gainer sent her a message that she would love to babysit tonight. Natalie deletes the message. She also snoops around Arpi's box. Inside is something very interesting that she received a week ago. It is from the agency's lead photographer. After reading the contents of the letter, Natalie knows she found another weakness.

Arpi,

*With every passing moment, I find myself thinking about you. I don't
know how you feel about me, but I don't care. When ever you bless me
with a taste of you, I am in heaven. Please tell me, what can I do to
have you again?*

James

Natalie even finds a response from Arpi.
James,

*You know how I operate. If you do for me, I will do to you. For the
sake of my career, I cannot become attached to anyone, you know this.
But as long as you keep opening doors for me, I will open myself to you.*

Arpi

A response from James.

*I have a contact within Cover Girl Industries. She is always looking
for fresh faces. If I can have you tonight, I will bring her to you.*

Arpi responded.

When and where?
James responds.
Studio B at midnight. Wear the blue cotton panties.
Natalie stops reading. She knows all she needs to know about
the situation and finds it humorous. Arpi projects herself as a
strong and intelligent woman, but she whores herself for modeling
opportunities. Natalie can use this to her advantage.

Natalie goes to the office kitchen and prepares a cup of coffee
for Raylene. She jazzes it the way Arpi showed her; strong regular,
three sugars, and one cream, just how Raylene likes it. As an
added bonus, Natalie snorts mightily and hocks a large loogie

into the cup. She stirs the drink to dissolve the phlegm and takes it to Raylene's office. She prints a copy of the expense report and leaves it on the desk, next to the coffee.

Retuning to the front desk, she sees the front door open, and Raylene walks in. She plays it cool, just like she rehearsed with herself last night.

"Good morning Miss Cordova." Natalie says.

"Good morning Natalie." Raylene answers nervously.

Natalie sits at her desk.

"Your coffee and the expense report are on your desk." Natalie begins. "Arpi came in and said she would return around 12:30pm."

"Very well." Raylene replies. "Write this down. I need you to reserve the conference room for me from noon until two. I have a meeting with Gerald Alexander about an opening in his firm. I need printouts of our operating statements dating back two years. Call AMR magazine. Confirm their commitment to pay Willow her publication bonus. They just crossed a million copies sold and need to pay up. Cross reference last month's numbers to two months ago, identify negative trends and get back to me. I'll need that analysis before my meeting. And e-mail Izzy. We got the contract for the Spanish men's magazine and her first shoot is tonight. Michael and I will be there to support her. Speaking of which, I am expecting an e-mail form a Ms. Gainer to babysit Dominique tonight. Let me know when that comes in straight away. Do you have all that?"

"Yes I do." Natalie answers. "Conference room from noon to two, AMR for Willow's bonus, find negative trends the past two months, info to you before noon, Izzy photo shoot tonight, viva la raza, and Ms. Gainer for babysitting. Anything else?"

"Not right now." Raylene says as she walks away.

Slave driver!

Natalie sits at her desk and takes to her duties. Hours pass and Natalie is bored out of her mind. All the tasks were done, Raylene got her numbers and reports, and Natalie had nothing to do. As she tries to fight boredom, the office door opens. In walks Willow, Ben, Michael, and Dominique. Willow sees Natalie sitting behind the desk and gasps.

"What the fu…" she says, catching herself, "fruit are you doing here?"

"I'm working here now." Natalie answers.

"On my God!" Willow exclaims. "That's awesome!"

She runs up to Natalie and gives her a hug. She squeezes the girl and sways her from side to side. Natalie returns the embrace. Michael sneaks up behind the two girls.

"This is a spot of good news." He says.

Natalie breaks her hug and looks at Michael.

"Sorry I crashed your party like that." She says.

"Don't even worry about it." He replies. "It looks like it all worked out. I'm Michael."

"Natalie." She says. "Very nice to meet you."

She looks down at Dominique and admires her.

"Hey there cutie." She says.

"Hi!" Dominique responds excitedly. "I'm Domi."

"Hi Domi." Natalie replies. "I'm Natalie."

In a rush of emotion, Dominique wraps her arms around her big sister. Natalie is surprised, but does not protest. She hugs the girl back and holds her tight.

"I was hoping I could meet you." Dominique says and gives her a kiss on the cheek.

"Oh," Natalie begins, "you are so sweet."

"Yes she is." A cold female voice cuts in from the other side of the room.

Raylene walks over to the group with a scowl on her face, not pleased to see her daughters interacting. She is in a foul mood, but Michael does not notice.

"This is great sweetheart." He says. "Look at your beautiful daughters. They look exactly alike."

"Michael, this isn't wha…" She begins but is cut off.

"I got a great idea." He says. "Domi and I just stopped by to say hi, but seeing how this is the scenario, let's all go to lunch. What do you think Domi?"

"Yay!" the little girl exclaims.

"Absolutely not!" Raylene blurts out loudly.

The others in the lobby are caught off guard by her tone and demeanor. Raylene lowers her head in embarrassment. Natalie can't help but enjoy her shame. Raylene's face begins to turn red as she fumbles with her words.

"I...uh," she begins, "um...it's just that...well..."

"She just got out of conference with a potentially huge contract." Natalie cuts in. "Could be worth millions in fact. Over two million a month and she said she needed me to help her get all the paperwork in order. You know, no time to waste."

Raylene turns her head to Natalie, surprised she attempted to make a save.

"Is that true?" Michael asks.

"Um," Raylene answers, "yes. Very true. We can't afford to lose time, so no lunch for us today."

"That's fantastic babe." Michael says. "I'm so proud of you."

"Thank you." She says faking a smile. "So if you will excuse us, we will..."

"Not so fast." Michael interrupts again. "I'm not wasting this opportunity. Natalie, Raylene and I have a function to attend to tonight. Would you like to watch Domi for us?"

"What?" Natalie asks in disbelief.

"Please?" Dominique begs. "Please? Please? Please? Please?" She repeats the word while bouncing up and down.

"I'd love to, but..." Natalie answers.

"Good!" Michael shouts. "Be at the house by 5:30pm."

"Michael," Raylene cuts in, "I will not have this."

"It'll be fine." He says. "Domi wants it, don't you baby?"

"Please mommy." Dominique pleads. "Pretty please?"

She hugs her mother and tugs on her shirt while begging. Raylene feels trapped and cannot refuse.

"Fine." She concedes. "Just this once."

"Yes!" Dominique shouts.

She runs over Natalie and hugs her.

"This is gonna be great!" She says.

"Come on Domi." Michael says. "We have to prepare for tonight."

The little girl gives her big sister a kiss on the cheek and leaves with her daddy, waving goodbye as she leaves. Willow is right behind them.

"Well I hope you're happy!" Raylene scowls.

"I was ambushed!" Natalie protests. "Obviously you didn't tell him I was working here. Had he known, he might not have shown up."

"What I tell my family is none of your business!" Raylene responds.

"It looks like it is now;" Natalie says. "seeing as how I'm now your babysitter for the night."

"Now don't you get any ideas…" Raylene begins.

"I'm not the one with ideas of a happy family." Natalie cuts her off. "Do you think I want to spend any extraneous time in your house if I don't have to?"

"Then cancel the babysit." Raylene demands.

"I can't!" Natalie replies.

"Why not?" Raylene asks.

"Because," Natalie begins, "for starters, you gave your consent. Secondly, you haven't gotten e-mails from that other lady, and third, you saw the look on Dominique's face. Do you really want to disappoint her so badly?"

Raylene is silent while contemplating Domi's potential disappointment.

"Look Ray," Natalie says, "I'll do a good job. I won't fill her head with ideas of me and her being best friends. She'll be fed and in bed by the time you get home. Afterwards, you can tell Mr. Wonderful that you just don't like the idea of me watching her. Or even better, you can tell him the truth."

"Okay, okay." Raylene stops her. "You've made your point. Just take good care of my angel and don't you dare let anything happen to her."

"You got it." Natalie replies.

"Alright." Raylene says. "It's 3:15pm right now. Leave now and change your clothes. Your have to be at my house by five."

"Alright." Natalie replies.

She grabs her handbag from her desk and clocks out.

"I'll see you tonight Ray." She says.

"Just go." Raylene replies.

When Michael and Domi arrive home, the little girl rushes upstairs. She wants to get pictures and her favorite dolls to show Natalie. She rummages through her room until her father walks in.

"Hold up sweetie." He tells her. "You don't grab anything until you get a bath towel. You're taking a bath first."

"But Dad," Domi protests, "she'll be here soon."

"And when she gets here, you're going to be nice and clean." He replies.

"Aw man." She pouts as she heads to the bathroom.

As usual, he helps her get undressed and runs her water. Her places her in the tub and places her clothes in the hamper. Taking his usual wares, he heads toward his office, but is interrupted by a knock at his front door. He opens the door and greets his visitor.

"Natalie!" he says in surprise. "Didn't think you'd be here until later."

"Ray told me to get a move on soon after you left." She replies. "I hope I'm not intruding."

"Heavens no." he answers. "Come right in."

He steps aside to let her enter the house.

"I'd love to give you a tour of the place," he continues, "but I just got an e-mail to join in on this conference call."

"No problem." She says. "If you could just point me to the nearest can, that would be great."

She tightens her legs and bobs in a mock potty-dance.

"Sure." He says. "The first door on your left down the hall, just past the kitchen. It's Raylene's private powder room. I'm sure she won't mind."

"Thanks Mike." She replies and heads for the hall.

She enters the powder room and shuts the door. After dropping her pants and undergarments, she sits on the toilet and empties her bladder. She had held it for almost the past two hours. After finishing, she washes her hands with soap and warm water.

Private powder room. Snoop around!

Quickly and quietly, she fingers the many drawers of the vanity. She finds makeup, applicators, tampons, douches, hair care products and other toiletries; nothing of interests. Sitting on the vanity was a jewelry box. Going through, she found the standard fare, diamonds, gold, rubies, and other precious metals and stones. She opens the top drawer of the box, and takes out a rather unattractive piece of jewelry. It looks like a pendant, small and bland. She can't figure out why Raylene would want to keep something so plain and ugly. As she moves the pendant around in her hand, she notices it leaves a white powdery residue on her fingers.

OH MY GOD!

Instantly, Natalie remembers the crying model in the dressing room, burying her sorrow in a pile of cocaine. Could this ugly piece of jewelry be the source? Using both her thumbs and index fingers, she tries to twist it. To her amazement, the pendant opens. She tilts it towards her pinky and some white powder comes out. She takes only a small amount, and rubs it on her gums. Within moments, her gums go numb. Not proof of cocaine, but definitely a drug of some sort.

SWITCH!

Natalie pours the rest of the contents of the vial into the toilet and flushes it down. She opens the cabinet under the sink and looks for some sort of powdered cleanser. In the middle of the spray bottles and bottles of bleach, she finds a canister and reads the label.

Duramax Caustic Soda Lye. Instantly dissolves any biological matter blocking drains. Industrial Strength. See Results in Seconds!
PERFECT!

Natalie pours a pile of the lye into the sink, and scoops some up into the vial, filling it up to the top. Afterwards she washes the rest down the drain. After cleaning the outside of the pendant, she places it back into the jewelry box. After taking a minute to touch up her makeup, she leaves the bathroom.

Back inside the main hallway, she heads to the living room. It is filled with ornate paintings and other forms of artwork. She sees all the signs of her mother's success and it makes her sick. She takes comfort in the fact that it will not last much longer. The front door opens and Raylene walks in.

She acknowledges Natalie's presence with a slight nod, then heads upstairs. She has to quickly change and get ready for tonight's shoot with Izzy. She reaches the master bathroom and takes a quick shower. Afterwards, the puts on her perfume, makeup, and an elegant pantsuit she chose to wear. When she is dressed, she heads back downstairs. She sees Michael in the living room, sitting on the couch and talking to Natalie. She enters her private powder room and locks the door. She opens a small drawer on her jewelry box and pulls out a bland pendant. She puts it on and returns to the living room.

"Are you ready Michael?" She asks her fiancée.

"Just one more minute." He says.

He returns to Natalie and points to a sheet of paper on the coffee table.

"This is my cell phone number," he begins, "contact me should anything go wrong. If, for some reason, I don't answer, call Ray on her cell. This is the number to Domi's doctor and the local emergency services. Any questions?"

"Just one." Natalie answers. "When is her bedtime?"

"Nine o'clock." He replies. "But tonight, I'll give her ten."

Ok, I'm all set." Natalie says. "You two kids have a great time."

"NATALIE!" A jubilant yell is heard coming from the stairs.

Dominique comes running down the stairs into the living room. She runs up to Natalie and throws her arms around her waist. Natalie hugs her back. She can't help but giggle at Domi's princess pajamas.

"I'm so glad you're here." The little girl says.

"Me too." Natalie replies. "Me too."

"Come here Domi." Raylene cuts in. "Give mommy and daddy kisses."

The girl goes to her parents and gives them each a big hug and kisses on the cheeks. Afterwards she goes back to her big sister.

"Have fun you two." Natalie says. "This little monkey's in good hands."

Raylene and Michael walk out the door, with Raylene taking one final look back. As soon as the door closes, Dominique engages her big sister.

"Come on." She says and tugs on Natalie's arm. "I wanna show you my room."

Natalie smiles and follows her little sister.

Seven-thirty in the evening and Raylene is mingling with the lead photographer. She walks through the concept of the shoot with him, inspects the props, and goes over different lighting elements. This will be Isabella's premiere shoot for this magazine and Raylene wants everything perfect.

"Must the lights be so damn bright?" She demands.

"I'll get them dimmed right away." An assistant answers.

"And what about the wind elements" She asks.

"The fans are being configured in the back." He answers. "They should be ready with the next 20 minutes."

"Good." She replies. "Make sure the fog rolls in gently. Hugging her body, and selling her goodies to the reader."

"Yes ma'am." He answers.

"Where is my little starlet anyway?" She asks.

"She arrived on set 30 minutes early," he answers, "and is in her dressing room. She is dressed and made up, but she is quiet and will not open the door for anyone."

"Oh, fuck me." Raylene mutters to herself. She walks toward the dressing rooms.

Dominique has spent the last 15 minutes jumping on the bed, while her big sister tosses little pillows at her. She laughs as each pillow softly strikes her.

"You gotta tire out sooner or later." Natalie says.

"Not until." Dominique answers.

"Not until what?" Natalie asks.

"Not until this!" The little girl exclaims, and pounces on Natalie.

"Aaaa!" Natalie shrieks and falls to the floor, catching her baby sister.

"Gotcha!" Domi shouts.

"No you don't!" Natalie replies.

Quickly, she flips over and pins Domi to the ground. Then the tickle assault begins. Domi throw her arms and legs up in a futile attempt to guard her tummy.

"Truce!" She yells in a fit of laughter. "Truce! Truce!"

"I'm not stopping 'til you turn purple!" Natalie replies.

Despite that promise, Natalie halts when she sees the little angel is short of breath. She backs up and lets Domi regain her composure. She waits until her kid sister sits upright and faces her.

"Let's review." Natalie begins. "You said, truce, truce, truce. That's a three second truce. One."

"No!" Domi shouts.

She bolts from the room, as another tickle torrent was only two seconds away.

"Two." Natalie continues. "Three!"

She takes off after Domi. Natalie toys with her for a few minutes, getting to within a few feet, only to smack her on the backside and let her go. This is a special time for her. She forgets all about her anger, and takes the time to enjoy her first few moments with her baby sister.

Isabella is a nervous wreck, as usual before major shoots. She has spent the last 15 minutes crying, trying to soothe her shattered nerves to no avail. Her leg trembles uncontrollably and the longer she sits, the more it shakes. Her chest and arms shiver, and she has broken into a cold sweat. She knows what she needs, but only one person can supply it to her.

Raylene opens the door to the dressing room and smiles at her beautiful model. Isabella returns the friendly smile, and watches her as she walks in. Ray takes her usual seat next to Izzy and takes her by the hand. Izzy leans in and gives her mentor a big hug.

"I'm sorry Ray." She cries. "I can't do it."

"Shhh." Raylene insist. "Of course you can. You've made it through all the rest; you'll do sensational on this one. I believe in you."

"I know." Izzy answers. "I don't want to let you down."

"Oh Izzy." Raylene replies. "I've never been disappointed in you. You've always come through when I needed you, shining like a diamond."

"Thank you." Izzy responds. "But I've always needed the…."

"Hush now dear." Raylene interrupts. "Not for long. I've kept my promise. After tonight, you re-enter rehab, and I promise, you will get your life back."

"But what about tonight?" Izzy asks.

"What can I do for you my love?" Raylene asks.

Izzy once again looks Raylene in the eyes, before looking away. After all these years and the multiple photo shoots, she is still too ashamed to come out and ask for what she needs. Raylene can read her like a book and does not hesitate. She grabs a nearby mirror and places it near her on the vanity. She then removes and unscrews the pendant around her next, and pours a large amount of the white powder on the mirror. She then slides it over to Izzy, who is crying harder.

"Whatever you decide," Raylene says, "I support you. And I love you."

Isabella wipes the tears from her eyes. She opens the drawer and pulls out a twenty dollar bill. After rolling it, she looks back at Raylene.

"One last time." She says. "Then I break free."

She puts the bill in her nose and snorts all the powder.

Dominique and her big sister sit on the couch and watch some cartoons on satellite television. She drinks a glass of milk and is eating a freshly baked batch of sugar cookies.

"Mommy says I should not eat these." She says.

"Why not?" Natalie asks. "I thought all good little girls deserve sugar cookies."

"We do." Domi answers. "But mommy says they'll make me fat."

"Now why would I want to make you fat?" Natalie asks. "Better yet, if you believed her, then why are you eating them?"

"Because they taste good." Domi answers.

"You're so young and sweet," Natalie begins, "you should always do what feels good; and eat what tastes good."

"What if mommy finds out?" Domi asks.

"Don't worry." Natalie reassures her. "This will be our little secret."

"Cool." Domi replies. "Hey sis, what do you think mommy is doing right now?"

"I don't know." Natalie answers. "I'm sure she's having fun. She's worked hard, and deserves all the things that are coming to her."

ACHOO! ACHOO! ACHOO!

Isabella sneezes furiously. After she snorted the pile of powder, the sneezing fit began. Raylene rubs Izzy's back, trying sooth her sneezes. For a quick second, Izzy separates her hands from her face, trying to get some air for another sneeze, and reality strikes. Her hands are covered in blood. They go back to her face as another sneeze rips through her.

"Oh my God!" Raylene gasps.

Izzy turns her head to face Raylene. Blood has been wiped all over her face, her eyes are shut, and her skin is burning red. She tries to respond, but a sneeze stops her, sending blood spraying onto Raylene's face.

Raylene jumps away from the sickly girl, and stands looking in horror. Izzy falls from her seat and tries to find Ray. She can't open her eyes because they burn. Her tears have been replaced with blood and she cries crimson tears. The caustic lye in her bloodstream has spread to her lungs and begins to eat away. Izzy gasps for air as it rushes from her body. She opens her mouth wide. The entire inside is chemically burned and her blood runs black from her mouth.

"Help...me...mom." Izzy pleads, but Raylene just stands in horror, unable to move.

Izzy starts to spasm, small twitches at first, but then become violent jerks. Her body turns red as the lye burns her blood and her veins become visible. She coughs hard as her throat fizzles, and more fluid erupts from within, splashing on Raylene's leg.

Izzy falls to the floor, and she is not responsive. The spasms continue, but she no longer makes any noise. Raylene steps forward slowly, tears streaming down her.

"Izzy?" She says tearfully. "Please wake up."

She places her hand on Izzy's forehead and raises her face. She looks her in the eyes and stares into the face of death. Izzy's eyes were completely red, and the liquid drains from her tear ducts. Her mouth is black and blue as dark blood pours out. With no clear thoughts in her mind, and no other recourse, Raylene screams.

Dominique fell asleep while watching a movie and Natalie carries her upstairs. She reaches the bedroom and places the sleeping girl in her bed. She tucks her in and kisses her on the forehead.

"I love you little sister." She whispers before leaving the room.

Heading back downstairs, Natalie is happy. Spending the evening with Domi brought her joy, and made her forget about her pain. Looking at her watch, she sees she had plenty of time before the parents came home. After cleaning up the kitchen and living room, she heads to Michael's study to surf the net, relax, and possibly find some dirt on her mother.

While waiting for the computer to boot up, she sees all sorts of bank statements on the desk, detailing the financial dealing of Michael's production studio and Raylene's agency. When the computer comes one, Natalie snoops around for a while. She finds contracts, agreements, legal forms, all sorts of boring documents. Pressing further, she finds folders containing modeling photos. She recognizes the usual suspects from the agency, as well as a few other girls. Looking through other folders, she is surprised to find hardcore pornography.

Michael's secret stash!

Natalie digs further into the porn folders, hoping to find something embarrassing or harmful to Raylene. She finds numerous file and photos of intercourse and threesomes, but the vast majority is fetish files, such as bondage & dominance, and slave & master. All pictures showed the woman in the dominant role. Looking further, she finds a file folder called "The Glory of Youth."

Ah! Teenie-booper porn, bingo!

She double clicks the folder and is surprised to find it password protected. Puzzled, she tries her hacking skills. She tries a variety of passwords including Raylene, Ray, Mike, young, yummy, etc.

Running out of options, she goes for a "Hail Mary." She types in "DMC," Dominique's initials. The folder opens. Natalie cracks the password. After seeing the contents, she regrets her persistence.

Police photographers were on the scene, snapping pictures of the corpse of Isabella De Oro. Raylene stood in a corner staring blankly into space, and Michael stood at her side, trying to console her. She is an eyewitness, yet she has not been questioned. Detectives stand by the vanity, going over every detail. They confiscate the mirror with the white powder residue and take blood samples from the victim. They take her jewelry, clothes, purse, and cell phone. The workers on the set are questioned, and sketchy individuals are detained. Finally, an officer comes over to question Raylene. He is a scruffy looking gentleman, looking to be in his 50's.

"Ma'am," he begins, "I understand you were here with the victim when this happened."

Raylene does not answer. Michael steps in.

"She hasn't said a word since she stopped screaming." He says. "She hasn't even moved. Izzy was one of her best models, and a good friend."

"I'm sorry for your loss." The officer responds. "I'm Lieutenant Jacob Pritchett of the L.A.P.D. I know this is tough, but I need to know about anything about what happened here."

Raylene is still silent.

"Ma'am," Pritchett continues, "in my quickly assumed estimation, your friend died of a drug overdose, probably cocaine. That's a wild guess, because I've never seen anyone react this harshly to it, which makes me think it was laced with something. I need to know about her contacts and friends outside of work. If we can find the person who gave her the drugs, they'll be charged with first-degree murder."

"Murder?" Raylene asks abruptly.

"So you are listening." He replies. "What happened while you were with her?"

Raylene has to quickly clear her thoughts. If the officer found out that she had supplied the cocaine, she would be charged with murder. Despite her mourning for Izzy, she had to lie and label her as a secretive user in order to protect herself.

"I came in here," she began, "to see how she was doing. She always gets nervous before important shoots. Normally I come, give her a hug and my support, and then she asks to be alone. After a few minutes, she comes out and goes to work."

"So how was tonight any different?" He asks.

She has to think fast.

"I came in," she continues, "and she was leaning over the vanity. She turned around abruptly, and I saw something fall from her face. It was then that I saw the drugs. I demanded to know how she could do this to herself, and how long it had been going on. She said she needed it to function, and I should be glad because she always did a good job. I told her, I wouldn't have this in my agency and she had to make a choice. She defied me, and snorted it anyway. I was about to walkout and cancel the shoot, when she started gagging. I tried to help her, but I didn't know what to do."

She resumes her crying.

"I should have knocked her away." She continues. "I should have grabbed her by the ears, and forced her away. She would still be alive."

Lt. Pritchett holds up his left hand. Dangling from his fingers is the neck chain and vial that contained the powered. Raylene's eyes grow big with fright.

"We found this on the desk next to her mirror." He says. "It looks like this is what the drugs were held in. We're gonna run it through the lab, check it for prints, hopefully it will lead us to her dealer. Have you seen this before Miss?"

She has to lie again.

"Yes." She says. "It's mine. It went missing from my jewelry box a few days ago. She must have taken it."

"This is yours?' He asks. "Really?"

She nods her head.

"And it went missing." He says. "Okay."

He tone is sarcastic.

"Is there anything else you'd like to tell me Ms…" He trails off.

"Cordova." She says. "Raylene Cordova. Izzy's boss."

"Cordova." He repeats. "Ok Raylene. Here is my card. I will be in contact with you. Please leave your information with Deputy Paul over by the door, and you are free to leave. I recommend you contact her next of kin."

"I will." She replies. "Right away."

He turns around and walks away. He heads to the nearby CSI, who stands over the body and shakes her head.

"You find anything interesting Mary?" He asks.

"Oh." She says. "Hey Jake. This had got to be one of the most disgusting things I have ever scene. And being form L.A. that says a lot."

"What do you think?" He asks.

"Until I get in there," she begins, "I can't tell you much, but here is my best estimation. She snorted the coke, and what ever it was mixed with, it began eating at the soft tissue right away. She couldn't have lasted more than five minutes, and they were possibly the most painful five minutes of her life. Any suspects?"

"Her boss is dirty." He says. "She knows more than she's letting on. I'll start with her."

"That's very likely." Mary replies. "Drugs, cash, sex, contraband; in this business it all flows like water."

"How long 'til we know more about Miss De Oro?" He asks.

"Not long." She answers. "We'll pull an all-nighter. I'll be ready and have something for you within the next three hours."

He checks his watch. Nine o'clock.

"Good." He says. "Let me know right away."

"You got it." She replies.

Natalie stares at the computer screen in disbelief. Her stomach turns and tears run down her face. Flashing on the screen before her are hundreds of pictures of child pornography. At least one naked child was in every photo, and none were any older than Dominique. Each shot depicts acts such as oral sex, intercourse, sodomy, and group sex. Natalie cannot hold her disgust and vomits in the trashcan next to the desk. She wants to turn the images off, but one image comes on the screen and makes her freeze and pause the slideshow.

In the picture, a young girl, no older than four years old, is on her knees, giving oral sex to a man standing before her. Her eyes are closed and her tears are clearly visible. This act is against her will. The man in the picture is Michael. He is forcibly holding the girl by the hair and appears to be scolding her, forcing her to do such a thing.

Natalie resumes the slideshow. The next few pictures show Michael further raping the girl vaginally and anally, ending in a climax on her crying face. Natalie vomits again and cries harder, wishing she could save the poor girl. Then, a horrible thought flashed through her mind.

DOMINIQUE!

She hurriedly goes through every photo, looking for any sign of her little sister. She finds more pictures of Michael with other girls, each time forcing them to pleasure him, but much to her relief finds no pictures with Dominique. Her relief is short lived however, as her conscience takes over.

Protection!

Natalie knows what that means. Against her wishes and desires, she had bonded with Domi, and would do anything to protect her. Michael must not be given the chance to abuse her.

How dare she!

Natalie's rages for her mother grew. She is engaged to a man who willingly rapes little girls, and her baby sister could be next on the list. Raylene has to pay as well.

She can't afford to rush this however. She has to bide her time, and that meant leaving Domi at risk. She hated to do it, but she knows she has to. She must wait for the perfect time to strike at Michael. She could only hope that Dominique would be safe until then.

Natalie empties the puke filled trash can and turns off the PC. All that was left for her to do was wait for Michael and Raylene to get home. She heads back upstairs and enters Domi's bedroom. Inside, the girl sleeps peacefully. Quietly, Natalie walks up to the beds and slowly lies down next to her. The girl stays asleep, but instinctually flips over and wraps her arms around Natalie. Natalie hugs her back and kisses her on the forehead. She vows to keep her safe.

In the car, Raylene is silent. Her clothes are still covered in blood, and her thoughts are jumbled. Michael is very upset with her. He heard the comments she gave to police officer, and knew she was lying. He saw her leave the house wearing that pendant, that she was in the dressing room long before the incident occurred, and that their was no argument. Unable to fight his thoughts anymore, he confronts her.

"Why did you lie about the pendant?" He asks.

"What?" She replies.

"The pendant." He says. "I saw you wearing it when we left the house, but you told the cop it was missing. Why did you lie about it.?"

"Now is not the time Michael!" She scolds.

"It's the perfect time!" he shoots back. "Izzy just died, possibly murdered, and you piss on her memory by calling her a thief?"

"I'm not doing this right now!" She yells.

"Fine, I'll do it for you." He replies. "You lied about the pendant, you lied about how long you were in the room, what are you going to lie about next?"

When she doesn't answer, he slams on the brakes and pulls the car to the side of the road.

"What is the meaning of this?" She yelps.

"That was your pendant the cop held up." He yells. "Were you Izzy's dealer?"

"Of course not!" She defends. "I would never do that to one of my girls."

"But I saw you wearing it when we left the house." He replies. "Why should I believe you?"

"You want to do this now?" She shoots back. "You; a man with more kiddy porn on his computer than a Bangkok bordello. You really want to have a conversation about integrity?"

He cannot reply and lowers his head.

"That's right." She says. "I know about your sick perversions and wanting of pre-teens and young ones. I could easily ruin your career and expose you for the sick bastard you are."

"Ray." He stammers. "You…you wouldn't risk…"

"I would." She continues. "And if I ever discover my daughter in those photos, I will. Even if I go down with you, I will see you burn for it. So like I said, I am not her dealer!"

"So you'll just take me down like that?" He asks. "I thought you loved me?"

"There's one power in the universe greater than love." She replies. "And that's leverage."

He takes a heavy breath. The secret he hard worked so hard to hide was known to her, but she kept the secret for him to gain leverage. For what reason, he didn't know, but nonetheless, he was grateful.

"Ok." He says. "I believe you."

He returns the car to the road and continues to drive home in silence.

Natalie wakes up abruptly when she hears the garage door open. She gets up from Domi's bed and looks out the window. She sees Raylene and Michael pull up and exit the car. She straightens the comforter on the bed, gives her sister one last kiss and heads downstairs. She reaches the entry just as the two enter the front door. She sees the disarray and bloodstains on Raylene's outfit and begins her inquisition.

"Oh my God!" She blurts out. "What happened?"

"Nothing." Michael cuts in. "Just an accident at the shoot, but everything is fine."

"Are you okay Ray?' She asks.

"She's fine." Michael answers. "She's just going to shower, kiss Domi, and try to sleep it off."

"Ok." Natalie says. "I'm just going to use the bathroom. I'll call a cab while I'm in there and I'll wait outside for it."

"That would be great" He says.

Natalie walks into Raylene's private powder room and leaves the door open a crack. When she disappears, Raylene approaches Michael.

"Don't tell anyone anything about tonight." She says. "The girls wouldn't be able to handle it. I'll tell them when I'm good and ready. You keep my secret, and I'll keep yours."

Michael sighs.

"Agreed." He says.

"Good." She says.

She gives him a small peck on the lips and heads upstairs. Michael heads for his office. Natalie, standing inside the bathroom next to the door, heard every word. Something happened, of that she is sure. But worse, Raylene knows that Michael is a pedophile and child rapist. This burns her to the core. She composes herself, calls a cab, and leaves the house.

The following morning, Arpi and Hera have arrived at the agency early. They wanted to discuss Hera's part of the new contract, and find out how Izzy's big shoot went last night. They sit in the main office, going over the numbers, and potential financial impact to Hera, when Willow enters.

"Hola chicas!" She belts.

"What's this?" Hera says. "Is this the Willow Carter? Greeting us without swearing?"

"Oh shit!" Willow replies. "My bad. I fucking forgot!"

"Come on in." Arpi says. "We're just going over how much Hera can make with this new Ford deal. We can go over your details too."

"No can do!" Willow says. "I've got to find the lost daughter."

"Natalie?" Arpi asks. "Why?"

"Are you shitting me?" Willow yells. "You didn't hear? Ray let her babysit Domi last night. Natalie might actually soften up the old lady."

"I thought that would be impossible." Hera exclaims.

"So did I." Arpi says solemnly.

"You sound slightly pissed." Willow tells Arpi. "Why is that?"

"Look," Arpi begins, "seriously Will, don't you get it? This girl could change who Ray is, make her lose focus on what's important."

"What's more important that her fucking family?" Willow asks.

"Us, you ignorant child!" Arpi barks. "If she softens and accepts this girl, then she could possibly decide to give less time to the agency. This place would fall apart without her and our careers would be in jeopardy."

"Who the fuck you calling an ignorant child, you paranoid bitch?" Willow shoots back.

"Don't be so naïve Willow." Hera cuts in. "Arpi's right. We could eventually lose everything. Natalie has already threatened to go public with this whole ordeal and she could rip apart all that we have worked so hard to gain."

"We'll I'll be damned!" Willow replies. "What happened to doing the right thing? What happened to the thought of a happy family reunion. You know, a happy Ray is good for business…"

"We can't risk that!" Arpi responds. "If she bonds with Natalie, she'll change. The effects would be unknown and I can't afford the unknown, not when I'm so damn close to my goal!"

"So this is all about you then?" Willow contends. "Your billion-dollar dream?"

"This is about us Willow." Hera says.

"Will you please shut the fuck up you spearchucker?" Willow yells. "Better yet, go tell Rafiki, Puumba, and Simba you miss them!"

"Willow, that's uncalled for!" Arpi shouts.

"I GIVES NOT A FLYING FUCK!" Willow roars. "You lied to me Arpi! Ever since we met, way back when in the hospital, I respected and loved you like a big sister. You said you'd always be there for me, yet every single cause I've believed in, you shot down' claiming it wasn't good for me. But now, the truth is out. You never cared about what was best or about what is right. Everything is about you, how you benefit, and how much money you make. You've pretty much been using me."

"I bonded with you in the hospital." Arpi states. "Yes, I felt sympathy for you, and wanted to do whatever I could to set you off on the right path. I did think of you as my little sister, but what did that get me huh? FIRED! That's what. I lost my dream of becoming a doctor, and struggled to eat for a solid year until Ray found me. I had to learn quickly, that the only person who matters in my world is me! I don't give a shit about some little bitch not seeing her mother in seven or some odd years, and I care even less about how you feel about it!"

Willow is stunned by Arpi's blanket honesty.

"Look at your contracts Will." Arpi continues. "Everything you do pays me! Every deal you sign, every time you smile, I get a cut, a big fucking cut! But you wouldn't know, because you're too damn stupid to read the fine print! That's why I was so eager to have Ray sign you, because pretty young girls like you, are dumb pieces are shit!"

Tears rush down Willow's face as Arpi confesses.

"Did you actually think I cared about your teenage ordeal?" Arpi asks. "I wanted you, so I could play you like a god-damn GameBoy. As far as I'm concerned, you should have let that guy take your fourteen year old cunt. Maybe you would have wised up, and realized that's all you're good for!"

Willow snaps. She tackles Arpi and drives her to the ground. Grabbing her former friend by the collar, she lands a punch to her face.

"I HATE YOU!" She screams.

Hera grabs Willow from behind and tries to lift her off Arpi. Willow lowers her face and bites down hard on Hera's arm. The girl yells in pain and lets Willow go. The raging model gets off Arpi and wraps her hands around Hera's neck. She hoists her up by the neck, places her on the hutch and slams her head against the wall mirror, shattering it. Arpi gets off the ground and tries to pry Willow away from Hera, and three-way struggle begins.

"FREEZE!" A male voice roars. "EVERYBODY FREEZE!"

The girls stop and look towards the voice. A large man in a trench coat stands by the door and holds a gun, pointing it at the models. They stand still, in fear of him.

"What's going on here?" He demands.

"Nothing." Arpi says quietly. "Just a…misunderstanding."

"Misunderstanding?" He asks. "You three about to kill each other over a misunderstanding?"

"Yeah." Arpi answers. "Simple right?"

"Separate!" He says. "One of you there, one there, and one there. Go."

He points to three different areas of the room and the women comply.

"Who are you?" Hera asks.

The man lowers the gun and reaches into his pocket. He pulls out a badge and shows it to the girls.

"You're a cop?" Willow asks.

"Lieutenant Jacob Pritchett." He replies. "I'll be asking you three tigers some questions. I'll need your names, first and last, age, and how long you've been working here. Let's start with you."

He points to Arpi.

"Arpi Tahmasian." She says. "24 years old. Working here for four years."

"You next." He says and points to the next girl.

"Willow Carter." She says. "18 years old. Ten months working."

"And you?" He asks and points to the final girl.

"Hera Williams." She says. "22 years old. Three years."

"Do any of you ladies know Isabella De Oro?" He asks.

"Yeah." Hera answers. "She's a model, like us."

"What did she do now?" Willow asks.

"She's got a history?" He asks. "A record?"

"Not a record." She says. "Just bad judgment."

"What happened, Lieutenant?" Arpi asks.

"Miss De Oro died last of an apparent cocaine overdose." He says.

"WHAT!" All three models shout in unison.

"I guess you boss hasn't told you yet." He remarks.

"What?" Arpi asks. "How? When?"

"Last night at her photo shoot." He answers. "We suspect the drug was laced which something, but we don't know what. So any help you ladies can provide would be helpful."

Arpi collapses against the wall and breathes hard; clutching her chest trying to get air. Hera has sat down and lowered her face into her hands as she cries. Willow stares blankly for a second before responding to the officer.

"Her private dressing room," she begins, "is through that door."

She points to a door behind him. He thanks her and heads inside. He spends about 20 minutes looking around, trying to find any information on a dealer, but comes up empty handed. He re-emerges back into the main office and sees the women now hugging each other and crying. He breaks their embrace to give his card to each.

"I'm sorry for your loss." He says. "If you can think of anything, please call me."

They nod in agreement and he leaves the office. Walking through the waiting room, he sees a young lady sitting behind the reception desk. She is a new face, so he decides to ask her some questions. He takes out his badge, and walks over to her.

"Excuse me Miss." He says and shows his badge.

She looks up from her computer screen and looks at the man. She wants to blow him off, but upon seeing his badge, he decides to cooperate.

"May I help you officer?" She asks.

"I'm conducting an investigation about an employee here." He answers. "Can you give me your name, age, and how long you've been employed here please?"

"Natalie Cordova." She begins. "19 years…"

"Cordova?" He asks and cuts her off. "Any relation to Raylene Cordova?"

"Yeah." She answers. "Biologically, she's my mother, but she won't accept me. I haven't seen her in seven years, and she shuns me."

"How is that possible when you work here?" He asks.

"We struck a deal." She answers. "She gives me a good paying job, and I remain hush-hush about our bloodline. Could be bad for business."

"How long have you worked here?" He asks.

"Today," she says, "would be my second day."

"Did you know Isabella De Oro?" He asks.

"I've heard of her." She says. "Only rumors though."

"What kind of rumors?" He asks.

"Talking about this to you won't get me fired will it?" She asks. "I mean, L.A. is expensive, and I've already told you too much about our arraignment, and if she were to find..."

"Miss Cordova," He cuts her off again, "Isabella De Oro died last night of an overdose."

"What?" She asks. "Oh my God, the rumors were true."

"Rumors of drug use?" He asks.

"Not just any drugs." She answers, "Cocaine. Some of the girls claim that she gets real antsy, and she snorts when she's depressed."

"Is that all?" He asks.

Natalie leans in close.

"I don't wanna risk my job," she says quietly, "can any of this be traced to me?"

"Not unless you get subpoenaed.' He answers. "But if you don't talk, you could get booked on obstruction of justice, and face charges yourself."

Natalie takes a deep breath and leans even closer.

"Rumor has it," she begins, "that Ray knew about it, and would supply it in order to get Izzy to calm down before big clients. I don't know if it's true, but that's what I heard."

"Anything else?" He asks.

'No." She says. "That's all I've heard."

He reaches into his pocket and takes out another business card.

"We'll be in touch Natalie." He says as he gives her the card. "I'm sorry for your loss."

He turns around and walks away. As soon as he exits the office, Natalie smiles brightly. She had guessed right, and took down her first target. She could not be happier. She figures that if a cop was here, he must have spoke to someone. She quickly erases her smile, puts on a glum face and heads to the back. She heads into the main office and finds the three remaining models.

They break their embrace and look at her. She forces her self to cry and plays along.

"Oh my God." She says. "So it's true?"

Willow gets off the ground, and runs into Natalie's arms. Natalie hugs her tight and lets her cry on her shoulder. Hera and Arpi look at the scene. Anger builds in Arpi, but she does not show it, however Natalie can sense it. She decides, Arpi will be the next to fall.

Raylene stays in bed this morning. She goes over the events of the previous night in her mind repeatedly, but cannot determine what went wrong. The vile she used was the same as usual, and no one had access to it other than her. The supplier was the same one she has used all year, and he only supplied her quality stuff. She could not try to lead the police to him, because he would lead them right back to her. She cannot afford to go to jail, and in her desire to keep her freedom, she does not mourn her fallen model.

Lt. Pritchett arrives back at the police station and heads to the autopsy room. As he walks in, he finds CSI Mary Howlett from the previous night, filing her morning paperwork.

"You didn't answer you phone last night." She says.

"Yeah," he replies, "I got home and the wife cut it off. You ready with your findings?"

"Follow me." She says.

The two officers head to the morgue where the carcass is kept. Upon entering, Mary opens locker 1284 and pulls out the sliding tray, bringing out a body covered by a sheet. She withdraws the sheet and reveals the corpse.

Isabella's face been cleaned of the blood, but was very sunken in. The skin was pulled tight and her facial bone details could be seen. Dark purple veins were visible all over her body and her eyes were dark red.

"Was it an overdose?" Pritchett asks.

"Yes and no." Mary answers. "Going through her blood work, she has a history and an addiction, but it's not what killed her.

We swabbed the vial we found at the scene. Only 0.002% was cocaine."

"What was the rest?" He asks.

"Right here." She answers and hands him a report.

He reads for a second then looks back at her.

"Caustic lye?" He asks.

"The tissues in the nasal cavity are very thin and delicate." She replies. "As soon as she snorted the lye, it immediately ate away at the membranes and tissues. As it entered her blood stream, it spread quickly through her body liquefying her capillaries. As the poison entered her lungs, her alveoli were instantly burned and she effectively choked to death. By then, the lye was spread throughout her body and continued to eat at our girl after her death, and continues now."

"Who would give this girl lye?" He asks.

"Don't know." She says. "But that's way you're paid the big bucks."

"Can't you give me any kind of lead?" He asks. "A brand or a manufacture?"

"When it mixes with blood," she says, "it's indistinguishable. I'm sorry lieutenant."

"Dammit!" He says.

He further curses under his breath before storming from the morgue.

By early afternoon, word of Izzy's death has spread through the entire agency. A makeshift memorial is set up in the dressing area and employees place flowers and candles in honor of Izzy's memory. Shoots are canceled or rescheduled to give grieving models time to mourn.

Natalie spends the day fielding phone calls from the press, and telling them to call later when Raylene would be in. She had consoled Willow earlier and convinced her to go home. Hera leaves soon after, but Arpi insists on staying. During her lunch break, Natalie walks in on Arpi, trying to call James, her photographer playboy, but he will not answer his phone. She breaks down once, because she needs someone to talk to, but she wants to be the strong one in the office. Natalie decides to take action.

She returns to her desk and accesses the email system. She signs in as James and composes an e-mail to Arpi.

Dearest Arpi,

I heard about what happened, and I feel terrible about it. How are you holding up? My heart hurts when I think about you in pain and mourning. What can I do to help ease your pain?

James

Natalie sends the e-mail. Within minutes, she receives a response.

James

I need you so badly right now. I know you're in Mexico right now, but I just need someone to talk to, and I was hoping you would be here for me. I tried calling, but you don't answer you cell phone.

Natalie replies.

Please forgive me. In my haste to make it to today's assignment, I broke my phone. But we are finished here. I'll be on the first plane back. Meet me at the agency, tonight at midnight.

Arpi responds
Won't that be too late for you after a trip?
Natalie replies.
I would wait for you forever, even at the gates of heaven.
A final response from Arpi.
I'll be here.

———

137

Natalie closes.
I'll be waiting.

The bait is set. All Natalie has to do is set the trap, but she has to get everyone out of the office before she can. She decides to gain permission for everyone to leave early. She picks up the phone and calls her mother.

"Raylene's not here!" A woman's voice roars on the other end.

"Ray," Natalie yells, "this is Natalie, from work."

"Natalie," Ray says, "What do you want?"

"Everybody here knows what happened to Izzy last night." Natalie answers.

"What?" Raylene yelps. "How? I never…"

"A cop came by this morning." Natalie says. "He spilled the beans to everyone."

"Shit!" Ray yells.

"Look," Natalie begins. "We got an office full of young women bawling and crying their eyes out. Shoots are getting rescheduled, models are doing nothing productive and getting paid for it, the press is calling, we have…"

"The press?" Raylene asks. "Who talked?"

"No one!" Natalie answers. "The cops must still be blabbing. Let me send everyone home. Nothing's getting done here, and sooner or later, someone's going to crack."

"Yes." Raylene agrees. "Close it down. Tell everyone to go home, but no one talks to anybody without addressing me first!"

"You got it." Natalie replies. "Bye."

Natalie gives Arpi the news, and word spreads around the suite. Within the hour, everyone is gone. Natalie and Arpi are the last people to leave. As they lock up the door, Natalie addresses her co-worker.

"Hey Arpi," she begins, "I know things have been odd lately, with me showing up and now this, but you and Willow said you wanted to be there for me. So, I want to return the kindness and be there for you. Anything you need, I'll get it or do it for you."

"That's sweet of you." Arpi answers. "Maybe we can talk more tomorrow. I'm gonna meet a friend tonight, and just hang out."

"Ok," Natalie replies, "we'll talk tomorrow."

The girls say their goodbyes and go their separate ways.

Hanging out, what a fabulous idea!

Natalie calls a cab and heads to a hardware store. She asks the cabbie to wait for her and keep the meter running if he has to. She enters the store and buys a bag of terry cloths and 40 ft of thin, but strong rope. Returning to the cab, she returns to her hotel room. She retrieves the bottle of chloroform from her belonging and changes into some different clothes. She waits patiently in her room until 8:30pm. She calls another cab and is taken to her office building. She walks into a small home store next to her job and buys as many little candles as she can hold. She leaves the store and goes to the studio.

She heads up the elevator and gets off on her floor. She heads toward her office, but walks past the door. Instead, she heads for the metal panel on the other side of the hall. She opens the panel and trips the circuit breaker for the office. Using a flashlight, she enters the office. She begins her preparation by strategically placing her candles to lead her victim to the catwalk above the main set. To ensure Arpi's temptation, she leaves little pre-prepared notes along the same path. When she reaches the catwalk, she takes her rope and fashions a noose out of it, and ties it to the rail. Finally, she goes to every portfolio and photo book she can find and takes out all the pictures of Arpi. She places the pictures in a box and sets it aside. She checks her watch one last time, 11:42pm. All she can do now is wait.

Arpi arrives at the studio at 11:50pm. Upon peeking her head inside the door, she sees the lit candles and smile.

"Ah, how sweet." She says to herself. "James?"

No one answers her. She calls out again but still to no response. She sees another candle, this time accompanied by a note. She reads the small note and smiles again. She takes off her shoes and continues to follow the path of candles and notes. With each note she reads, she moves a little faster. She calls out a few more times, but each call is unreturned. She finds one last note, leading her to the catwalk above the main set. She climbs the ladder without hesitation and reaches the top.

On the catwalk, there were more candles, but no notes.

"James?" She calls again. "Where the hell are you?"

Her call is returned this time, by an arm clamping around her chest from behind and a hand pressing hard against her mouth and nose. Arpi struggles initially, but cannot fight for long. The towel is soaked and the fumes from the liquid are making her very dizzy and short of breath. After only a few moments, she blacks out.

Later…

Groggy and still dizzy, Arpi slowly stirs on the floor. Her eyes throb and feel heavy. She tries to rub them, but cannot. Her hands are bound behind her back. She jerks at the sudden realization, but cannot scream because she is gagged. Her eyes shoot open and she gauges her surroundings. She remembers that she is on the catwalk and was here to meet James. She blacked out and now she is bound and gagged. She begins to panic and fear for her safety. She begins to wiggle her wrists, trying to pry her hands free, but the duct tape is wrapped tight and will not allow it. She unleashes a muffled scream for help, but the tape covering her mouth makes her inaudible.

She hears footsteps, and jerks her head up. She expects to see a dangerous man emerge and her eyes well in fear. Instead, she sees Natalie emerge from the shadows, and feels a sudden rush of relief, as if help has arrived.

"Oh my God!" Natalie exclaims and runs over to Arpi, kneeling beside her. "Arpi. Are you ok?"

Arpi shakes her head no.

"Good." Natalie replies.

Arpi's eyes shoot open at Natalie's response. Before she can process what has happened, Natalie jumps to her feet and boots Arpi dead in her stomach. Arpi screams through her gag and pants hard through her nose. Natalie does not stop. She repeatedly kicks at Arpi's soft midsection, trying to damage as many organs she can. Arpi can't breathe, as every breathe is cut short by another kick. Natalie changes her focus from the abdomen to her ribs, and breaks a few in the process.

Arpi writhes in pain as the blows never ends. She pants through her nose, desperate to get some air. The kicks stop for a quick moment, before a swift kick plants her in the mouth, breaking some of her teeth. Her mouth fills with blood with no place to escape. Natalie then kneels directly on the girl, placing her knee on her neck and pressing hard. Arpi feels her throat close as the air is cut off. Her vision starts to go dark and her movement slow. The blood in her mouth rushes into her throat and she feels she will drown, when the pressure is suddenly released. The air forcibly rushes into her nose and down her throat. Her breathing is so haggard, she shoots blood from her nose as her air returns.

Natalie reaches behind her victim and retrieves the noose. She drapes it over Arpi's head and tightens it, barely allowing Arpi to breathe. Afterwards, she reaches to the back of her pants and retrieves her hunting knife. She holds it front of Arpi's face and enjoys her terrified reaction.

"When people find you now," she begins, "they will know exactly, what you are."

She takes the blade and places it to Arpi's forehead. The traumatized girl lets out another muffled scream as Natalie carves "BITCH" into her face. After admiring her work, she lifts Arpi off the floor and sits her on the rail of the catwalk.

"Any last words?" Natalie asks and rips the gag off Arpi's mouth. The girl can only scream.

Natalie calmly shakes her head no and pushes Arpi over the edge. Arpi screams during the freefall, but only for a second. The rope reaches it limit and jerks the girl before she can hit the floor. The violent force snaps her neck. Arpi is killed instantly and her lifeless body swings just over the floor of the set.

Natalie is not yet ready to savor another kill. She leaves the catwalk and heads to the set to finish her work. She retrieves the box of photos she has amassed and dumps them on the floor underneath Arpi's corpse. She then gets a chair, places it next to the pile and stands on it. She raises her blade and buries it inside Arpi's chest. Holding firm to her knife, she jumps off the chair and rips the blade downward, tearing it through Arpi's chest and abdomen. After landing, she withdraws the knife and shreds a horizontal slice across the girl's belly. After a few more rips and tears, Apri's entrails flush from her body and land on the bloody pile of pictures beneath her feet.

Satisfied with a job well done, Natalie traverses the office and gathers her knife, and the bottle of chloroform. She leaves the office and returns the power. Outside the building, she does not call a taxi. She walks the distance back to her hotel, smiling the entire way.

The Saturday morning sun shines through the bedroom windows, and sends a dull pain into Raylene's mind. She did not report to her office yesterday, and doesn't anticipate this being a pleasant weekend. She reflects on the events of Thursday night as she lay alone in her bed. Michael was gone, having taken Dominique to her dance lessons. Raylene contemplates spending the day in bed, when the doorbell rings.

Grumbling as she moves, she puts on her robe and heads to the front door. Opening it, she feels her day will get even worse, as Lt. Pritchett stands waiting for her.

"Officer Pritchett." She says. "What brings you here?"

"I figured you would use Friday to grieve." He answers. "But I hope you understand, I have an investigation to run, so I need to ask you some questions."

"Of course, "she replies, "please, come in."

She steps to one side and he enters her home. He takes a second to observe his surroundings before heading for the couch in the living room.

"Can I get you some coffee?" She asks.

"No thank you." He answers. "This should be quick."

He takes a seat and she sits net to him.

"I need to know about Isabella De Oro's background." He says. "What was she like, and what kind of work did she do before you signed her?"

Raylene takes a deep cleansing breath.

"Izzy was a lost soul when we met." She replies. "I met her at a fundraiser for the mayor a few years ago. I thought she was part of the youth voter initiative. In reality, her father disowned her after she served time for a reckless driving charge. Being a talent scout, I just thought she was gorgeous. I gave her a screening and signed her afterwards. She used the money she earned to improve her living situation and one day return to school."

"When did this reckless driving charge occur?" He asks.

"Oh my!" She answers. "I think it was about three years ago."

"That's strange." He replies. "Because I did find a charge against her three years ago, but it was for drug possession. Cocaine to be exact."

Raylene swallows hard, she does not like where this is headed.

"I was unaware." She responds.

"I also found out," he continues, "that she was entered into a rehabilitation facility, about 15 months ago, paid for by the Femmes-Jolies Modeling Agency. Now, maybe you can explain to me how you were so surprised to know about her drug addiction when only a short time ago..."

"Listen to me!" She cuts in. "Izzy was a scared little girl who needed someone to take care of her. Yes, I knew about her addiction, but I put her in rehab like any responsible adult would. I tried to help her."

"Then why lie about your knowledge of it" He asks.

"I didn't want anyone to know," she answers, "because I was trying to protect her reputation, and my business. The girl had such a hard life after her parents abandoned her. I just wanted to do what was best for her. Please, you have to understand."

"I'll understand," he says, "once I am sure I'm getting the truth out of you. Were you her supplier?"

"No." She answers. "I swear I was not. Her falling back into addiction was my worst fear. I know what we do is very stressful, but I hoped she was strong enough to resist."

Pritchett's phone rings. He excuses himself so he can answer it.

"This is Pritchett" He says. "Good, what have you got?… Really?…Yeah I'm here…Yes, she is…Alright, we're on our way."

He hangs up.

"What's going on?" Raylene asks.

"Ms Cordova," he says, "you need to go to our bedroom and put some clothes on. We have a field trip, you and me."

From the look in his eyes, Raylene knows that she should not ask any questions. She excused herself to get dressed. Afterwards, they got in his car and left the house.

The Femme-Jolies Agency is a madhouse. Earlier that morning, emerging model Stacy Clears arrived to gather some garments she wanted to use for a shoot later in the week. On her way to the dressing room, she passed the first set and screamed an ear piercing shriek. A janitor cleaning the halls heard the bloodcurdling siren and ran to her aid. He too saw the sight and almost froze in horror. After a few seconds he carried the still screaming girl out of the office and called the police.

At ten-thirty this morning, Lt. Pritchett and Raylene pull up to the curb next to the building. Squad cars are in full force and the press is quarantined away from the scene. Pritchett leads Raylene into the building and they ascend up the elevator.

"What's going on?" Raylene demands. "What's happening?"

"I don't know." Pritchett answers. "We're both about to find out."

The elevator stops at the 40th floor and the two depart. Raylene fears they found something linking her to Izzy's death. She does not have time to process her options when she and Pritchett are approached by a woman.

"Jake." She says. "Sorry about the short notification."

"No problem." He replies and points to Raylene. 'This is Raylene Cordova. She's the founder of this joint."

The woman extends her hand to Raylene, who shakes it.

"Hello Ms Cordova." She says. "I'm CSI Mary Howlett."

"CSI?" Raylene asks. "Does this have something to do with Izzy?"

"We don't know." Mary answers. "I need you to see something, but I warn you. It is very disturbing, graphic, and will be very hard to view. I'll take this time now to apologize in advance."

"What's going on here?" Raylene ask.

"Follow me please." Mary says.

Howlett, Pritchett, and Raylene walk into the agency. Immediately, Raylene sees the candles on the floor and her curiosity builds. As they get further into the agency, more candles, and a few scraps of paper can be seen. The reach the entrance to the first set and stop.

"Ms. Cordova." Mary says. "Please brace yourself."

Howlett opens the door and the imagery strikes like a jackhammer. The body of Arpi Tahmasian hangs above the floor of the set. Her face is caked in dried blood, her eyes are lifeless and sunken within the sockets, her neck is bent at an awkward angle and her skin is flash pale. Most disturbingly, her abdomen is ripped open and she has been gutted. Her entrails hang from her corpse and leads to a pile of photographs on the floor. Raylene takes in the sight for one second before she loses control.

"ARPI!!" She screams.

She lunges forward, towards the body. Howlett and Pritchett move quickly to try and restrain her. They each grab one of her arms and hold her back. She fights their grip and tries to move forward, screaming the whole time. Pritchett is able to get a hold of her and lift her out of the studio. Other officers converge on the hysterical woman and Pritchett lets her go. A medic rushes over and injects her with a sedative. Within a few seconds, she slowly blacks out and loses consciousness.

Pritchett wipes the sweat from his brow and rejoins Howlett in the studio.

"Fuck me." He utters under his breath.

"I'm sorry about that lieutenant." Howlett says. "But we needed a positive I.D."

"A positive I.D?" He asks. "This is a model agency. You couldn't just grab an album and find out who she was?"

"We tried." She answers. "All the albums are missing her pictures. The only photos we could find are in that pile of intestine underneath the body. Maybe you'd like to disturb the crime scene and take one."

"How long until you're done processing?" He asks.

"A few hours." She answers.

"Shit." He mutters as he walks away.

He walks towards the body and looks at it the face. The killer obviously took liberties at beating the victim. Both of her eyes were blackened and a few of her teeth were missing. The coup de grace was the word "BITCH" carved into her forehead.

"Mary." He calls out. "What name did she say?"

"Sounded like Arbay," she answers, "or Arpy, I'm not to sure."

He repeats the name to himself and takes out his notepad. He flips through it until he finds his notes from yesterday morning. He reads them then gives a name.

"Arpi." He says. "Arpi Tahmasian. I came by here yesterday and met her."

"Anything of merit we can use?" She asks.

"Maybe." He says. "When I got here she was in a fight with two other girls. Their names are Willow Carter and Hera Williams. Get them in here. Let's see what they know."

"Alright," she replies, "we'll get someone on it."

Raylene wakes up at her desk in her office a few hours later. While initially groggy, she quickly realizes where she is. She looks across her desk and sees Lt. Pritchett on the other side.

"Officer." She says.

"Are you alright Ms. Cordova?" He asks.

The events of the morning flash in her mind.

"No." She answers tearfully. "Who could do such a thing?"

"We are trying to find out." He replies. "Raylene, I need you to tell me everything. First Isabella two days ago and now Arpi last night, in your own studio. This can't be a coincidence. Either someone is coming after your girls, or coming after you."

Raylene clears her mind. She can't lie anymore.

"I knew about Izzy's addiction." She begins. "I supported it. It was the only way she survived the major shoots for our clients. We tried rehab, but it didn't work for long, and old habits die hard. She just had one last shoot to go. We secured another client, and needed to deliver a stellar spread. She promised me, that after it was done, she wanted to return to rehab. I even made the arrangement for her to start today. I had no idea she would react to the cocaine the way she did."

"It wasn't cocaine." Pritchett cuts in.

"What?" She asks. "Of course it was. I've been buying it from the same man for 6 months without issue."

"We ran trace on your pendant." He says. "It wasn't cocaine, it was caustic lye."

"Lye?" She asks "That's impossible! Why would someone want to snort that poison?"

"Who did you buy it from?" He asks.

"I don't know his name." She answers. "I just meet him every two weeks on the UCLA campus; by the Basketball gym."

"What happened when you made the last purchase?" He asks.

"It was a week ago." She says. "He told me he was raising the price by double. I said that was fine because this would be my last time buying from him. He got angry, but I told him to get over it, paid him the money, then he reached in his pocket and gave me the stuff. That was it."

"Sometimes," Pritchett cuts in, "these guys will switch the product if they feel they're getting slighted."

"But how would he know this would be my last purchase?" She asks.

"He probably didn't," He answers, "but he had the lye with him anyway. When you pissed him off, he may have just made the switch. Where can we find him?"

"I wasn't his only customer." She says. "He is at the gym every other Friday. Any other time, I'm not sure of. Do you think he could have anything to do with Arpi?"

"I don't know." He answers. "It's possible, but we won't know until we bring him in. Until then, some of our other investigators may have more questions for you. I'm going to keep you in this office until we move the body. When we are all finished up, we will take you home. If you cooperate with us, we will not pursue any drug or murder charges."

"I'll cooperate anyway I can." She replies. "Thank you."

Natalie wakes up late Saturday morning and she is full of mixed emotions. Arpi is dead and she is achieving her goal in quick order, but instead of jubilation, her thoughts continue to flash to the images on Michael's computer. She decided to be patient in dealing with him, but after only a little more than 24 hours, her patience has run out. She can't help but fear that her sister is being molested this very second. She has to do something.

Natalie calls a cab and heads for a seedy part of Downtown Los Angeles. She finds an ATM machine and takes $500.00 out of her account. Back in the cab, she rides past a sleazy looking motel. She gets dropped off on a street corner about a block away and walks back to the motel. She walks to the front desk, asks for a room, and pays cash for it. Just as Natalie wished, the clerk took no information. Once she got the key, her next destination was a hardware store.

Raylene was allowed to make phone calls while sequestered in her office. Her first phone calls were to Michael, Hera, and Willow. Hera and Michael remained strong, but Willow was a wreck and couldn't finish the phone call. Raylene was able to get them to agree to meet on the 42nd floor on Monday, and together handle arrangement for funerals of Arpi and Izzy.

Natalie has learned to appreciate hardware stores. She always found fun and exciting items she could use creatively. While walking the aisles, she grabs a hot glue gun, a power drill with bits, and black spray paint. After her purchases are complete, she heads back to the motel.

Michael returns home with Dominique later in the day. He has not yet told her about Arpi, and will leave that to Raylene. After his phone call with Ray, he decided to go home and wait for his fiancée so he can console her and dry her tears. He sends Dominique upstairs so she can play while he figures out how he will handle this. His doorbell rings, much to his surprise, and he answers the door.

A crying Hera stands on the porch outside the door. He welcomes her in and gives a big hug to comfort her.

"I'm so sorry Hera." He says.

"How could all this happen?" She asks.

"I don't know." He answers. "But they'll find who did this. I promise"

He leads her to the couch so she can calm down. He goes to the kitchen and gets Hera a glass of water. Upon bringing it to her, the phone rings. He answers is expecting Raylene.

"Ray?" He says. "How you holding up?"

"This isn't Ray Michael." A woman's voice responds.

"I'm sorry." He hays. "Who is this?"

"Michael," she says, "I know all about you."

"Excuse me?" He asks. "Who are you?"

"I know what you've done." She says. "The little girls. The photo files. The glory of youth."

Michael goes cold. Someone else knows his secret.

"All the kids you've raped," the woman continues, "I know. I know how you like it, how you need it, and how your woman protects you."

After a lengthy pause and more taunting by the caller, Michael responds.

"What's this going to cost?" He asks.

"Just your presence." She replies. "Tonight, at the Piazza motel on Slauson at 8pm. Room 24. Come alone, no cops, and do not leave me waiting."

The caller hangs up. Michael wipes the cold sweat off his brow before turning to Hera on the couch. He checks his watch, 7:20pm. He has to get moving.

"Is everything ok?" Hera asks.

"Um," Michael responds, "no. Looks like a production company wants to sue me. I know this is short notice, but could you do me a favor?"

"Yes." She answers. "Anything."

"I have to meet my attorney about this in 20 minutes." He says. "Can you stay here and watch Domi while I'm out?

"Sure." She answers. "No problem. Where is she?"

"She's upstairs playing." He replies. "I really appreciate it."

He grabs his car keys and heads out the door.

At 7:30pm, Raylene is finally able to leave the studio. She is emotionally drained and physical spent. All she wants to do is get home and hold her daughter. She knows she'll have to break the news to her, but she doesn't know how. She gets on her phone and calls her home.

"Hey Ray." A woman on the other line says.

"Who is this?" Raylene asks.

"It's me, Hera." The woman says.

"Hera my dear." Raylene replies. "I'm so sorry. Is Michael there?"

"No." Hera replies. "He got a phone call from his attorney. Some production company is trying to sue him, so he went to meet his lawyer."

"Damn." Raylene says. "So I assume Domi is with you."

"Yes she is." Hera replies. "We'll be here waiting for you to arrive."

"Good." Raylene says. "I'll be there in a few minutes."

Michael arrives at the destination and parks his car. He is very unsure as to whether he should be here or not, but he cannot allow for his actions to reflect poorly on his future wife, or his daughter. He locks the car and heads to the room. Climbing the stairs, the finds room 24. He knocks on the door and it opens a crack. He pokes his head inside and inspects the room. It is standard fare for a sleazy motel, complete with a small television, full size bed, small bathroom, and a tiny closet.

"Hello?" He calls out.

No response. He steps inside and closes the door behind him. He calls out again, but still no response. He takes another couple of steps and his contact emerges.

Michael feels a heavy weight jump on his back and a hand covers his mouth. A wet towel is pressed over his face and the fumes are heavy. He does not last long, and after only a minute, he is out cold.

Natalie loves her chloroform.

Raylene is at her home. She greets Hera and Dominique in the living room. Together, the women break the news of Izzy's and Arpi's death to Dominique. They try to sweeten the news as much as possible, but the young girl cries heartily anyway. As Hera hugs the sobbing girl, Raylene receives a text message on her phone from Michael.

Leaving for New York. Back in a week. Love you.

"Oh hell no." Raylene stammers.

She dials Michael's cell number, but he does not answer. She checks the time and leaves a voice message, demanding he call her back.

Michael lifts his groggy head. He is sprawled on his back in a motel bed. He tries to get up, but his hands are bound to the headboard. He yanks and struggles hard, but the ties do not loosen. He looks down at his feet and sees that they too are bound to the base of the bed. He cannot call out for help because his mouth is gagged. He lays still and looks around. This is when his focus returns. Looking at the ceiling, he sees the word "PEDO" painted in black.

He scans the room and finds the word painted everywhere, on every surface. The door, walls, and even the TV screen were covered in the word. He tries to calm down, but he begins to panic. Closing his eyes, he breathes steadily from his nose. He feels his breath traverse across his chest and begins to relax; then realizes that he is naked.

A toilet flushes. He shoots his gaze over to the bathroom, in the direction of the sound. He stares in fear, as he waits to see his captor emerge. The door opens and Natalie walks out.

Michael is stunned. He murmurs loudly through the gag, trying to protest his situation. She doesn't acknowledge him, just walking towards him and kneeling at the side of the bed. She stands back up, holding an extension cord. She unfurls it and in one swift fluid motion, whips him across the abdomen.

He screams into the gag, writhing in pain. The sting of the strike is intense, and burns throughout his entire body. After his initial reaction, she whips him again. This strike lands across his chest. It was a harder, faster strike, and it splits the skin wide open. A third strike had the same effect on his abs and a fourth lash, the fiercest of all, lands across his groin, slashing his thighs and bruising his penis.

Michael's body feels as if it is on fire. His skin burns hot, yet he can still feel his blood ooze from the wounds inflicted. He writhes uncontrollably, hoping the air will cool his burning skin. Natalie stops after the fourth strike and plugs in the extension cord. She reaches under the bed and pulls out the drill she purchased earlier in the day. Michael sees the drill and struggles mightily, yet futile, against his restraints. She plugs in the device and pulls the trigger, paying no attention to the terror Michael feels. She straddles his right calf and immobilizes his leg. To keep him still, she holds her knee on his ankle, and violently drives her foot into his groin. Slowly, and deliberately, she drills the bit in Michael's right knee.

He screams with all his strength and feels every centimeter as it boroughs through his patella and into the soft meaty mass of his knee ligaments. Natalie pushes the entire length of the ¼ inch wide drill bit through his knee. She smiles as it punches through the other side. Fueled by his muffled screams and the splattering of his blood, she reverses the drill and just as methodically, withdraws the bit. The blood rushes from his knee and pools on the bed.

She unplugs the drill and reaches under the bed again. She pulls out her hot glue gun and lets it warm up. She says nothing, just leans against the wall and closes her eyes. She remembers the images on the computer screen, of Michael raping those poor children, and her anger intensifies. She wants him to feel the pain she felt, as she stared at those images.

After a minute, she grabs her gun and inserts a glue stick. She holds it over his neck and squeezes the trigger very slightly. Much to her delight, the hot glue oozes out and drips onto his adam's apple. He writhes again as the heat eats into his skin. Natalie doesn't waste any of her resources. Only a drop falls on his neck. She repositions her self over his chest and begins to pour. His screams encourage her actions and she scribes the burning glue onto his bare skin. She stops when she is done and admires her work, the word "PEDO" scrawled across his upper body in hot glue.

Michael's eyes are bloodshot, and his face is red; wet with tears. He does not know how much more he can endure. He is lightheaded from the loss of blood from his knee, and is ready to give up. He stares into the eyes of his attacker as she readies the cord to whip him again. She lands a strike across his face, gashing him on his left cheek. She then wraps the cord around his neck and cuts off his air supply. As he writhes on the bed, struggling to gasp for air, she leans in close and whispers in his ear.

"Izzy was first," she began, "because she was Mom's favorite little pet project, and I've never cared for crack heads."

Michaels' eyes grow large with surprise at Natalie's confession.

"Arpi tried to replace me," she continues, "and Ray let her do it. So she had to go."

Michael begins to quiver, but still tries to listen.

"Hera is naïve," she continues, "and she won't even see it coming. But I do like Willow. She would make a good pet. She's just like me, yet Ray loves her, and not me, her own daughter. So she will die last."

She gets off the bed and releases the restraint around Michael's neck. He breathes heavily as he sucks in the air through his nose. Natalie reaches behind her back and retrieves her knife. She holds it to Michael's face.

"But you," she says, "are the sickest fuck I have ever met! You deserve this, and you will never get a chance to hurt my sister."

She thrust her arm downward and drives the blade into his right shoulder. She gives the blade a hard twist, and drinks in his screams of pain through his gag. As he squirms, she leans in one last time.

"And when you're gone," she says, "you won't be around to protect your woman."

She torques the blade and drives it from his shoulder across his chest. She withdraws the knife stabs repeatedly at his chest. She stabs him multiple times, splattering his blood with every strike. Michael cannot fight as he feels his life slip away. His vision goes from blurry to white, before fading to black. He dies.

Natalie does not stop. She continues to tear and slash until she cannot lift her arms. His ribcage is clearly visible when the slashing ends and she is covered from head to toe in his plasma. She lowers her head and smiles to herself, knowing her sister is finally safe.

Monday morning is taxing on Raylene. She had spent the previous day speaking to police, writing statements for investigators, and trying to contact Michael. She tried his cell phones without success, and even called the hotel he usually stayed at in New York. She became worried when she discovered he had no reservation made. Although she has yet to hear from him, she puts him to the back of her mind. She has to hurry to make it to the office. She has to meet Hera and Willow on the 42nd floor to make funeral arrangements for Arpi and Izzy. She calls Benjamin to pick her up from home, and checks on Domi. Since Michael is out of town, she has to take her daughter to school herself.

Dominique sits quietly on her bed. She is dressed for school, but looks very sad and cries. Raylene hurries to her bedside.

"What's wrong my darling?" She asks her weeping daughter.

"I miss daddy!" Domi cries. "He left without kissing me goodbye."

"Oh sweetie." Ray response and she hugs her daughter. "He was just in a hurry. I'm sure he thought he would come back that night. But you know how hectic his work gets."

"I know." Domi replies. "I also miss Arpi and Izzy."

"So do I sweetie." Ray says. "So do I."

They remain silent for a minute before the young girl speaks again.

"Mom?" She asks. "When can Natalie come over again?"

Raylene sighs. She does not know how to answer.

"Honey," she begins, "we have other things that we need to think about; other than Natalie. She'll come over when she can. I promise."

The little girl continues to cry as her mother holds her.

Natalie arrives to the building at 9:00am. The police are still there, going over investigation records, and looking for any missed clues. A few of the officers voice their frustration and find themselves in a dead end. Natalie uses all her focus to avoid smiling. She heads to the elevator and ascends to the 40th floor.

Exiting the elevator, she sees the hallway full of cops. One looks at her and is puzzled. The officer, a female in her 40's walks over to Natalie.

"I'm sorry ma'am," the officer begins, "but this floor is closed."

Natalie turns on some fake sadness.

"I know." She replies. "I work at the agency, and no one's called me or anything. I saw all this on the news, and, I just wanna talk to somebody from the office. I want to know what's going on. How could this happen?"

The tears rolling down Natalie's face sells the cop on her sincerity.

"Hey, hey." She says. "Don't cry. I promise, as soon as we know what happened, you and everyone from the office will know. Until then, we'll keep you safe."

"Thank you." Natalie replies.

"You welcome." The officer responds. "There were some of you co-workers here earlier. They said they would be going to the 42nd floor to meet with their boss. They should be up there. I'm sure you can talk to them."

"Thanks." Natalie replies as she walks away.

Getting back on the elevator, she pushes the button for the 42nd floor. She has heard of the additional administrative space Raylene began renting there, but she has yet to ever see it. This would be a first for her. The elevator arrives and Natalie departs.

She steps out into the hallway and finds it deserted. The hallway is decorated with the same carpet and wallpaper as the 40th, just with zero cops.

"Hello?" Natalie calls out.

After a few seconds, Natalie hears a door open and footsteps come towards her at a running pace. After another few seconds, Willow emerges from around the corner. She looks terrible. Her face is reddened from crying and wet from nonstop tears. Her eyes are bloodshot, as if she has not slept in days. Her clothes are tattered and wrinkled and her hair is tossed and unkept. She looks at Natalie and solemnly approaches her.

"Oh Willow." Natalie says and heads toward her.

The girls meet and wrap each other in an embrace. Willow buries her face in Natalie's shoulder and cries a little harder. Natalie squeezes her tight and lightly strokes her hair. She turns on the tears to further sell her concern.

"I'm so sorry hun." Natalie says. "I'm so sorry."

"I was so wrong." Willow replies. "I'm fucking horrible!"

"Whoa, whoa," Natalie interrupts, "now wait a minute! What are you talking about?"

"The last thing I said to her," Willow begins, "was that I hate her. I don't hate her, but now I can't make it right."

"Now don't think about that." Natalie replies. "I'm sure she knew that you didn't mean it. You girls were like sisters, and that's just the type of BS that sisters do. She knows you loved her."

"I was such a bitch." Willow tearfully says.

"Okay." Natalie cuts her off. "That's enough. Let's go sit down."

She keeps her arms around Willow's shoulder, and follows the girl to an office down the hall. As they enter, Natalie sees Hera inside, talking on a cell phone, and she is not happy.

"What don't you understand?" She yells. "Am I not speaking English?"

The conversation continues.

"How much clearer can I be?" She asks. "Haven't you been watching the news? One of our models was brutally murdered! You know, Arpi Tahmasian! I have to get her affairs in order tonight. I can't do the fucking shoot!"

A short pause.

"DON'T YOU HAVE ANY FUCKING COMPASSION?" She screams tearfully.

She takes a second to calm her nerves.

"Fine." She says. "I'll take postponement until six o'clock tonight, but understand that this is not right."

She hangs up her phone. She sits down and scowls, trying to relax and cool her temper. She glances up and sees Natalie and Willow standing in the doorway. She addresses Natalie.

"Sorry you had to see that." She says.

"It's alright." Natalie replies. "It's just amazing, that even in a time like this…"

"Business waits for nobody." Hera says.

She walks over to the two girls and they have a group hug. Willow has calmed down a bit and Hera slows her breathing.

"I know these past few days have been terrible," Natalie begins, "and I just showed up at the worst possible time. Things have been awkward, but please, let me help out in anyway I can. I know you will be very busy making arraignments, so if I can make it any easier, please let me know."

"We need that." Hera says. "Thank you. It would help if I could get out of this United Nations Charity shoot."

"Charity shoot?" Natalie asks. "What's it for?"

"It officially protests the civil war in my country." Hera answers. "Nigeria. I'm supposed to portray a mother having her baby taken away. I'm on my knees and held at gunpoint."

"Sounds pretty powerful" Natalie replies.

"It is. "Hera says. "And I was very much looking forward to doing it. Hell, I insisted on it. But I never thought all this would happen."

Willow breaks away from the huddle of women and heads to a chair. She curls her knees up to her chest, holds them tight and cries to herself.

"Is she gonna be okay?" Natalie asks.

"I hope so." Hera answers. "She's been like this all morning"

"Is there anything we can do?" Natalie asks.

"No." Hera answers. "She's been like this before. It was right after her father died. Four months before you came along. The only person who could get her to open up and return to normal was Ben."

"Is he around?" Natalie asks.

"He'll be back soon." Hera answers. "He left about 20 minutes ago to pickup Raylene."

Willow whimpers and lowers her heads. Her tears can be seen rolling down her knees, on the inside of her thighs, and dripping onto the chair.

"Hey Natalie." Hera says. "Can you do me a huge favor?"

"Anything." Natalie answers.

"I have to go down to the garden level," Hera begins, "and get the props I need for the shoot tonight from storage room 17. I can't leave Willow like this."

"What do you need?" Natalie asks. "I'll get them."

"Thanks." Hera replies. "It's all in a plastic yellow tote labeled Hera: UN Nigeria, with today's date. It has a fake machete, military fatigues, a prop gun, some tattered clothing, and a baby doll."

"Okay." Natalie says. "I'll be back in a few minutes."

Natalie walks over to Willow and kisses her on the top of the head.

"I'll be right back." She says. "You gonna be okay?"

Willow nods her head while wiping away tears. Natalie gets up and walks into the hallway. Halfway down, she looks up and sees Raylene, Domi, and Benjamin turn the corner. Domi drops her mother's hand and runs toward Natalie. Natalie squats down and gives the girl a big hug.

"Hi big sister." Domi says.

"Hey cutie." Natalie replies. "Hey, can you do me a big favor?"

"Yup." Domi replies.

"Willow is very sad" Natalie says, "and needs some love right now. Can you go give her the biggest hug you've ever given anyone?"

"I will." Domi replies.

She gives Natalie a kiss on the cheek before running the rest of the way to the office. Shortly after she leaves, Ray and Ben approach Natalie.

"Raylene." Natalie says.

"Natalie." Raylene responds in a shaky voice.

Natalie turns her attention to Ben.

"Hey Ben," she begins, "Willow is real broken up about, everything. Why don't you go see if you can cheer up while I talk to Ray for a quick second."

Raylene does not protest.

"Okay." He says. "Sure."

He turns to leave, but Natalie stops him.

"Hey." She says. "You look like a cop."

"I am a cop." He replies.

"I know that." She says. "But she's been questioned nonstop by cop after cop after cop. Don't you think you should walk in as Ben the boyfriend and not Ben the cop?"

"What do you mean?" He asks.

She lowers her eyes and shakes her head slightly.

"Take off the badge," she says, "and the belt with the spray, baton, and gun. I'll hold on to them for you."

"I can't do that.' He protests. "It's against protocol to give…"

"This is for Willow." She interrupts. "Isn't she worth it?"

"Of course she is." He says. "But I can't just…"

"Take them off!" Raylene demands. "Natalie's right. Willow needs you, as a confidant, not a cop."

Ben pauses for a second, then takes off his equipment and hands it all over to Natalie. Afterwards, he heads down the hall and enters the office. When he disappears, Raylene and Natalie face each other.

"Ray." Natalie says. "Mom. I know things have been extremely difficult these past few days. I'm sorry, I really am."

"I appreciate your sympathy." Raylene replies.

"Look." Natalie continues. "This whole thing, the whole situation I've imposed on you, just seems so minute now; and unimportant."

"I agree." Raylene says.

"I want to help you guys today." Natalie goes on. "Anything you need, I'm here for you."

"Okay." Raylene replies. "Thank you."

"And by tomorrow," Natalie says, "I'll leave your life; forever."

Raylene's eyes widen at this new revelation.

"I can admit that I was wrong." Natalie continues. "I had no right to pen you in a corner. You made decisions, you felt were necessary, and I should accept that. So I will leave tonight. You'll never have to see me again."

Raylene does not know how to respond. After all that has happened, she was not expecting to be free of her oldest daughter. Natalie turns and continues down the hall.

"Natalie!" Raylene calls out.

Natalie turns around and looks at her mother.

"I'm sorry I could not give you want you wanted." Ray says. "But this is the right thing. Thank you."

Raylene disappears into the office.

Natalie enters the elevator and descends to the garden level. Her thoughts are running wild. The police are much more persistent in Los Angeles than in Oregon, and she can't help but feel her time is running out.

Tonight's the night!

She has languished in this hell hole long enough, and playing the role of supportive daughter is more than she can bear. In order to get at Raylene, she would have to cut corners. Hera has a photo shoot tonight, so she would be out of the way. Unfortunately for Natalie, that also means that Hera will live.

Bigger Picture!

The bigger picture is how she can get at Raylene. As she exits the elevator and enters the storage room, she accepts that she will have to let one of her targets go. She finds the box in which Hera referred to, and digs through it. After a few seconds of checking props, she freezes.

"Oh hello!' She says to herself.

She pulls out a prop and gets excited. It was the fake handgun Hera mentioned, and it looks similar to Ben's. She pulls it out of the tote and sets it aside. She puts down Ben's belt and withdraws his gun. The items were not just similar, they were exact copies! Thinking quickly, she switches them. Before placing the real gun in the tote, she checks it and turns the safety off. Although she knew this would probably not affect Hera all that much, at least Ben would be less equipped to defend Willow and Ray.

Back in the office, Ben tries to calm his love while Hera and Raylene go over funeral services.

"This looks like a beautiful service." Hera begins. "It's done in a Catholic Armenian church in Glendale. I think Arpi would like that."

"She would love that." Raylene replies. "But we can't have a service for Izzy there, can we?"

"No." Hera answer. "But if we move Izzy's service up a day, we can get 'Our Lady of Guadalupe' in Inglewood. I know that Izzy wasn't deeply religious, but her family was so, maybe that would be appropriate."

"She was always a believer." Raylene says. "Yes, I think we can do this."

"HOW THE FUCK AM I SUPPOSED TO RELAX?" Willow screams at Ben.

All eyes in the room turn to Willow.

"Willow, calm down." Ben protests. "I'm just saying, you have to be strong, and prepare to face life without them. And if you need anything, I'm here for you. That's all."

"YOU'RE MAKING FEEL LIKE SHIT!" She roars back.

"Well if you let just let me…" He tries to comfort her, but she slaps him hard.

"GO AWAY!" She shouts before lowering her head once again.

Ben stands still in stunned silence. He doesn't know what to do anymore. After a moment, he turns around and walks away. Hera and Raylene both stand up and walk over to Willow. Raylene puts her arms around her, like a mother would.

"I know that this is very hard my dear," she begins, "and despite how much I may be hurting, I can't even imagine how horrible you feel."

Willow wipes her wet teary face.

"Try to imagine," Willow replies, "if you ever lost one of your daughters. How would you feel?"

Raylene pauses for a moment. She never even considered how she would feel if she lost Domi. The mere mention of the possibility cuts her life a dull knife to the heart. She is not upset however, as she tries to be understanding of Willow's question.

"If I ever lost Dominique," she replies, "I imagine that the pain would be unbearable, and I may not ever recover from it."

"Welcome to my world!" Willow states.

She gets out of her chair and storms out of the office. Slamming the door behind her, she heads aimlessly down the hall, not even noticing a visibly angry Natalie standing next to the doorway.

She heard her mother's reply. She swore she would not get attached or emotionally involved, but hearing Raylene's response was still devastating. Not once, did she hear her name mentioned. Raylene still refused to accept her oldest daughter, and Natalie could not prevent her tears from falling.

Kill her!

Natalie hears the voice in her head, but the thought is nothing new, and it brings her no comfort.

Kill the daughter!

"What?" Natalie says to herself.

This thought is truly horrifying.

Kill the daughter!

"What?" She says again. "No. I can't."

Kill the daughter!!

"No!" She repeats, and begins to cry harder. "Not Domi. I won't do it!"

Raylene's joy and happiness!

"But I love her." Natalie cries. "She loves me."

She replaced you!

"It wasn't her choice." Natalie protests.

Ray chooses her! Ray loves her!

Natalie's mind is spinning and she is not in control. Her thoughts focus on Domi, and she feels the love grow in her heart.

But her love for Domi, hastens her hate for Raylene. She knows that eliminating Domi will utterly crush Ray. But she can't bring herself to want to do it. Or can she? During her time in L.A, she has found love and a piece of her lost youth in her little sister. She desperately wants to cause her mother pain and suffering, but at what cost? Could she kill her sister in order to do that, therefore hurting herself? How much is she willing to sacrifice to hurt her mother?

"I…" she stammers. "I…I can't….I don't know…Domi?"

KILL HER DAUGHTER!!!!

"NO!" She screams and pulls her own hair.

The office door swings open and Ray enters the hall, wondering what the scream is about. She sees Natalie curled on the floor, pulling her hair and crying.

"What is going on out here?" Raylene demands.

Natalie shoots her gaze upwards and sees Raylene standing over her. She takes a quick look around, and remembers where she is. She rushes to her feet and wipes her face.

"Sorry Ray." She says. "I guess, all that's happened has finally hit me."

Raylene lowers her head and gives it a sympathetic shake. She reaches out and places a hand on Natalie's shoulder.

"Look." She says. "I'm touched, that you feel emotion for what we have lost, but don't you dare freak out now. My daughter looks up to you, and you have to be strong for her, just for this one day before you leave. Please, just do that. It's all I ask."

With that statement, Raylene re-renters the office. Natalie is silent with disbelief. To her face, her mother only acknowledges Dominique as her daughter; no regard given to Natalie, or concern shown for her own grief. Natalie balls her fist and looks down at the ground.

"Kill her daughter." She murmurs to herself.

Hera walks out into the hallway, just as Natalie has finished gathering herself. She sees the tote and is relieved that Natalie found it.

"Can you do my one last favor Nat?" She asks.

"Sure." Natalie says. "What's up?"

"My ride to the shoot is downstairs and waiting." Hera says. "Can you help me bring this down?"

"Yeah." Natalie says.

Each girl grabs a side of the tote and carry it downstairs. Outside the building, waiting at the curb, is a man sitting in a car. They take the tote and load it in to the backseat of the car.

"This shoot is all the way down in San Diego," Hera says, "so I have to get going now. See you later okay?"

The two girls hug and Hera gets into the car. After she buckles her seat belt, the driver takes off rapidly down the street. Natalie takes a second to sulk. She wanted to kill her, but sometimes, she does not get what she wants.

Natalie heads back inside the building and waits. She has no timeframe on when to execute her remaining targets. She decides just to wait, until the time is right.

Two hours and thirty minutes pass, and Hera is finally exiting the freeway. She and her driver have been speaking during the whole trip. She begins to smile as she begins to feel a little better. She knows that now is not the appropriate time to flirt with someone, but she partakes anyway.

"I'm glad to see you smile finally." He tells her.

"It's easy to do right now." She replies.

"Now," He continues, "how can I make you laugh?"

"You know," she answers, "I don't feel much like laughing, but you are free to try."

Her cell phone beeps abruptly. She looks down to examine it, and distress settles in.

"SHIT!" She yells. "We're running late! Can we go faster?"

"Are you gonna laugh for me?" He asks.

"What?" She yelps "Laugh?"

"I go slow until you laugh." He answers.

She gives a light chuckling gasp, and strikes him across the shoulder.

"Just drive you bastard!" She shouts.

He presses the pedal to the floor the car rockets forward. The set was just down the street, about fifteen minutes away. As the speedometer climbed to 80 mph, they darted through the intersections, making every green light. He glances toward the sidewalk and sees a "DIP" sign.

"Hang on." He says.

The car barrels through the intersection and takes the dip at full speed. The front end stays grounded, but the tail end hops off the street, sending the contents of the backseat air born, When the rear comes back down, disaster strikes.

BANG!

The driver turns his head toward Hera and slams on the brakes. The car comes to a complete stop, and he stares in horror. Hera sits back in the seat, taking short, quick breaths. Her chest is red, her shirt is covered in blood, and the plasma is spread all over the dash board and windshield. In the middle of all the blood is a small smoking hole, in the middle of the glove compartment. Hera clutches her chest as the blood flow increase to heavy. Her gasps shorten, she becomes dizzy, and her vision goes dark. She is lung shot.

"Oh…my…god." She pants.

Her eyes roll upwards and her heads slumps to her left shoulder. She dies. In a panic, the driver grabs her cell phone and dials 911.

Hours pass, and the day gives way to twilight. Raylene and Ben have been gone for quite sometime, looking at potential funeral sites for Arpi and Izzy. Willow was told to stay in the office, and Natalie was charged to watch over both her and Domi. The young girl came down with a bad cold and was sleeping in an adjacent office. Natalie has been talking with Willow the whole time, trying to get her to relax, and lower her guard. Her efforts finally began to bear fruit. The two girls sit together and watch television. Willow is still saddened, but is no longer crying. She just sits with her head slumping onto Natalie's shoulder.

Strike now!

Natalie's psyche speaks to her. This would be a perfect time to strike. With Domi asleep in the other office, Natalie could dispose of Willow. She would then return to take care of Domi. She can then leave the corpses in place for Ben and Raylene to find. She could then, finish the job. She gets a twinkle in her eye as she looks at Willow. It would be so easy for her to grab the bitch by the throat and choke her until she turns blue. She licks her lips in anticipation, but a special report on the news interrupts her thoughts.

"We interrupt our regularly scheduled program to bring you this special news bulletin from Channel seven, Eyewitness News. Good evening, I'm Maria Vega. We have some new information on that horrible shooting that took place in San Diego. Apparently, the driver and passenger were carrying a loaded gun in a yellow container in the backseat of the vehicle. The driver was speeding down the street when he hit a dip at the intersection of Longwell and Harvey. The impact from the dip set off the weapon and shot the young woman through the lungs. We are being told now, that the name of the victim is Hera Williams, a young and promising model from Nigeria. Police also report that the driver had no knowledge of the weapon, and they are baffled as well. We will have more on this tragic event as more details unfold. For channel seven, Eyewitness News, I'm Maria Vega, we will now return you to your regularly scheduled program."

Natalie sits in stunned silence. She cannot believe her luck. The gun she removed from Ben's belt, ended up killing Hera. Natalie is overjoyed and wants to shout her exuberance to the world, when Willow breaks her joyous mood.

"NO!!!" The horrified girl screams.

Willow jumps from her seat and runs out into the hallway. Natalie reaches the end of her mental rope with her. Willow is weak, whiny, unstable, and at this very moment, vulnerable. She gets up and heads out of the office as well.

In the hallway, Willow pulls on her hair and cries louder. She paces the hall, punches the walls, and kicks the trash cans. Looking up, between cries, she sees Natalie, just standing and staring at her. She approaches her friend, in desperate need of comfort. Natalie has other ideas.

When Willow is within range, Natalie rears back with her right hand, and unleashes a fierce backhand strike across Willow's face. The weeping girl falls to her backside and recoils on the floor. The stinging pain of the slap is burning into her cheek. She turns to face Natalie, her eyes begging for an explanation. Instead, Natalie grabs her by the throat, hoists the girl off the floor, and pins her against the wall, cutting off her air supply. As Willow fights to breathe, Natalie leans in close.

"This must be my lucky fucking day." She growls.

Willow is confused, and tries to pry Natalie's hands away.

"Izzy and Arpi were easy." Natalie continues. "Their fate was never in doubt."

Willow's eyes grow large as she listens to Natalie.

"W…w…what?" She stammers.

"I got to Michael too." Natalie goes on. "The police haven't even found his carcass yet. I must be lucky, because I was willing to let Hera go. But, I guess we both know what happened."

"You bitch!" Willow chokes. "You fucking bitch! Quit playing around"

"Famous last words." Natalie replies. "But you still don't get it."

She rears her arm and punches Willow in the gut. The girl gasps as all the air leaves her lungs at once. Natalie throws her on the ground and kicks her in the stomach. Willow writhes in pain on the floor. Natalie reaches behind the hem of her skirt and withdraws her knife. Willow's eyes grow large as she sees the blade. She knows that Natalie was not lying. She rolls onto her stomach and gathers herself to her knees.

"Oh." Natalie says. "You gonna run now bitch? I'll give you a head start."

Quite the opposite of what Willow had in mind. Willow vowed long ago to never be a victim again, and she is not about to change now. Instead of running, she lunges at her attacker, burying her shoulder in Natalie's stomach. The violent tackle forces Natalie to drop the knife and lose her breath. The girls tumble to the floor, and Willow lands on top. She mounts Natalie and lands two punches to her face, both to the left eye. Natalie reaches up and shoves three fingers down Willow's throat, causing her to choke momentarily and cease her attack.

Willow rolls off and quickly gets to her feet. As Natalie tries to stand from the floor, Willow buries a swift kick to her stomach. Natalie recoils and rolls away. Willow follows, grabs two handfuls of Natalie's hair, and violently yanks her off the floor, then slams her head against the nearby wall. In the next motion, she spins Natalie around, still by the hair, and throws her through a set of double doors, into an empty office suite. Natalie flies through the air and lands hard on her back, before rolling a few yards away from the door.

Natalie is in disbelief. The weak and feeble Willow Carter is beating the shit out of her. She is dizzy and every inch of her body throbs painfully. She feels tremendous pain in the back of her head, and feels her blood trickle from the open wound. She has very little time to think, as Willow approaches and once again grabs two fistfuls of her hair. As she is being pulled off the floor, Natalie thinks quickly. She twists to her left and lands a vicious uppercut to Willow's jaw. The girl's teeth crash together and Willow falls backwards. Her adrenaline rush has made her numb to pain, and she is back on her feet, minus three teeth. Natalie swings wildly and connects on Willow's jaw. She charges forward and pins Willow against a pillar. She drives her knee into Willow's gut and grabs her throat, trying to choke her. Willow tries to pry her attacker's hands away and jams her thumb into Natalie's left eye. Natalie stumbles backwards, but keeps her vision of her target. She goes back on the attack, but is stopped short, when Willow plants a punt right to her groin. Doubled over in pain, Natalie falls to the floor.

Willow does not stop. She grabs Natalie off the floor and slams her head onto a nearby desk. Picking the girl up, she does it again. Natalie head spins faster, and she is on the verge of losing consciousness. Moving fast, she grabs Willow's arm, and brings her hand to her mouth. She bites down hard. Willow grunts and tries to yank her hand away. Natalie bites down harder and draws blood. Willow shrieks and tears her hand away, leaving a piece of her flesh in Natalie's maw.

The taste of blood sends Natalie's senses racing. She feels renewed and re-energized. With this new clarity, she makes her fatal strike. Reaching to the side of the desk, she grabs a ballpoint pen. She hears Willow approach and she strikes. Natalie spins quickly, wildly flailing the pen towards Willow. The swing connects, and Natalie feels the pen penetrate into the moist, fleshy folds of Willow's right eye socket.

Willow falls to the ground, clutching her eye and screaming like a banshee. Natalie takes this opportunity to end the brawl. As Willow is hunched over, trying to remove the pen, Natalie steps in and punts Willow flush in the face, driving the pen into Willow's brain. The young girl flies backwards and lands on her back, twitching uncontrollably. Natalie falls backwards and leans heavily on the desk. Willow is done for. She knows this, but wants to be sure. Calling on what's left of her strength; she lifts a CRT computer monitor from the desk, and slams it down on Willow's head, crushing her skill. The body stops twitching, and Willow dies.

Natalie falls to the floor, thoroughly exhausted. Her body is ravaged, beaten, and bleeds from multiple orifices. She is glad that Willow is dead, but she asks herself if the effort was worth it. Her actions are soon confirmed. In the midst of the surrounding silence, Natalie hears a phone ring. Looking up, she follows the sound, trying to pinpoint its origin. The ringing is coming from Willow's pocket. Natalie retrieves the ringing phone and reads the Caller ID: Cordova, Raylene.

Finish this!

Natalie fights all her bodily pains and stands up. She stumbles to the door of the suite, leaning heavily on the wall. She enters the bathroom and washes up as best she can. Her black-eye and facial abrasions are clearly visible, but none of those matter. She has her next target in mind, and despite how painful her ordeal with Willow was, she knows her next step, will be the most painful she has ever taken.

On the freeway returning from Glendale, Raylene hangs up her cell phone. She leans back in her seat and turns to Ben who is driving her around.

"She's not answering her phone Ben." She says. "I tried."

"That's good." Ben replies.

"How is that a good thing?" She asks.

"It means she's not avoiding me." He answers. "Either that, or I'm not the only one she's avoiding."

Raylene chuckles at his coy, boyish remarks and turns on the radio to the local FM station.

"We have terrible news out of San Diego today. We just learned that local model Hera Williams, was shot and killed this afternoon."

"WHAT?!" Ray and Ben shout. They listen to more of the report.

"It happened earlier this afternoon. Police are reporting that Hera and her driver were transporting a loaded gun in their cargo. They hit a dip in the road and the weapon discharged, fatally puncturing Hera through the chest. Police have no..."

Raylene shuts off the radio, tears streaming down her cheeks. All the events of the past few days have flashed through her mind; Izzy cocaine sabotage, Arpi's hanging and disembowelment, Michael's sudden disappearance, and now Hera dying. All this happening too fast for her to handle and her poise begins to crack. She hyperventilates as she begins to panic. Her breathing is fast and shallow, and she turns red. The car spins around her and she cannot focus. Ben pulls the car to the side of the freeway and tries to get her to calm down. He grabs her hand and tries to talk her down.

"Come on." He says. "Stay with me, don't lose it now."

"I...can't...I..." She stammers.

"Think of your daughter." He says. "Be strong for Dominique. She's gonna need you."

Raylene closes her eyes and tries to gather herself. She calms little, but enough to collect her thoughts.

"Get me to my daughter." She cries. "I need my daughter."

Ben throws the car in gear and takes off toward Los Angeles.

Natalie digs in her purse and finds the small vial of sodium pentobarbital. She took from Ben's house. Looking further, she also finds the syringe. Taking the items, she heads down the hall to the office where Domi has been sleeping soundly for the past few hours. Slowly, Natalie approaches the little girl. Her knees are shaky and legs weak, but she proceeds forwards. Upon reaching Domi, she kneels down next to her.

Domi is sleeping on three large pillows and under a thick comforter. She breathes deeply and even snores a small bit. Lightly, Natalie takes her hand and brushes the hair away from her sister's face. The child whimpers, shrugs slightly, and slowly opens her eyes.

"Hey big sister." Domi says.

Natalie smiles.

"Hey there my love." Natalie replies.

Dominique rolls over and throws her arms around her big sister. She gives a firm squeeze and a loving embrace. Natalie winches in pain. She tried to hide it, but Domi squeezed in the right place.

"Ugh." Natalie groans.

"Are you hurting Natalie?" Domi asks.

"A little bit." Natalie answers. "I fell down the stairs earlier, but I'll be fine. How are you doing baby?"

"My tummy hurts," Domi answers, "and my throat is sore."

"You poor thing." Natalie replies. "It'll be okay. I've got good news sweetie."

"What's that?" Domi inquires.

"Mom gave me the name, number and address of your doctor." Natalie answer. "I went there and got some medicine for you. It'll clear up that cold in no time."

"That is good." Domi replies. "Can I have some please?"

"Are you afraid of needles?" Natalie asks, and holds up the syringe.

"Na-uh." Domi answers and hold out her arm.

Natalie takes out the vial, sticks in the syringe, and extracts the toxin. She takes the ribbon out of Domi's hair, and ties it around the girl's upper arm. She begins to cry softly as she inserts the needle into Domi's vein."

"Don't cry." Domi says and smiles.

"I'm sorry." Natalie says. "I just don't like seeing you sick, and suffering. I guess I should be strong, like you."

"Once your medicine makes me better," Domi replies, "I won't be sick anymore. Instead, I'll be pretty, like you."

Dammit!

"Oh!" Natalie cries.

She holds the needle in Domi's arm and hesitates. The poor dear offers no resistance, and only smiles at her big sister. Natalie's heart is ripping apart and her emotions run wild. She doesn't know if she can go through with this. She takes a deep breath.

"Domi." She says "I love you so much. I just want you to know that."

"I love you too sis." Domi replies.

Natalie holds her breath and bites her bottom lip. With a heavy heart, she injects the toxin. Domi's fate is sealed.

Dominique curls up next to her sister and closes her eyes. Natalie sits upright and strokes Domi's blond hair. She is stoic, not saying a word or uttering a sound, just listening to her breathe; and waiting. This is the longest and most painful moment she has ever known. Each second feels like an hour; each minute is an eternity. Domi's breathing slowly gets quieter and slower, but she never wakes up. Unconsciously, Natalie places two fingers on Domi's wrist, and feels the beat of her pulse. Each beat feels like a knife in the heart. She wants to scream; to extol her torment, but she can't; not as long as she feels those beats. It is a double-edged sword of emotions. She cherishes each pulse, wanting to hold one to each one, if only it could extend life for just a little bit longer. But each beat also feels her with dread; knowing it may be Domi's last. She does not keep time, just waits. Without warning, the beats stop and Domi falls silent. She dies peacefully her sleep. Natalie screams.

Lt. Pritchett arrives at the Piazza motel. He cannot shake the thought that Raylene and her husband know more about the murders than they let on. Earlier this morning, he assigned one of his rookie patrolmen to shadow Michael's car. It was found in the parking lot of the motel, but Michael never came out. After 10 hours of zero activity, the patrolman went inside. The clerk behind the desk did not have a record of anyone named Michael Milton. The young cop asked to see records of all registered guests and counted the keys remaining against the register. The clerk was one key short. The officer demanded to be let into that room. The clerk obliged; not wanting any trouble with the law. Once the door was opened, the officer radioed in for assistant.

Lt. Pritchett surveys the scene and feels the dread build in his stomach. He is tired of finding dead young ladies and fears he will find another. After clearing his thoughts, he heads up the stairs to room 24. CSI Mary Howlett stands in the doorway, blocking his path. She stares her colleague in the eye for a quick moment before dropping her head. A tear runs down her cheek.

"This just gets more and more fucked up." She stammers. "We're always a day late and a dollar short."

"What's her name?" He asks.

"Not her." Mary replies. "Him. It's Milton."

"What?" He snaps back. "It can't be him. He's one of our prime suspects."

"Well I guess he was innocent." She says. "In that regard, at least."

"What does that mean?" He asks.

"Follow me Jake." She replies.

He enters the room right behind her. There is a flood of CSI in every square foot of the room. Jake can barely get around, but he does take notice of all the graffiti sprawled on all the walls and windows, along with the foul odor of death.

"It fucking stinks in here." He says to himself. "The guy was a pedophile?"

"And apparently," Mary cuts in, "that's way he was killed."

Mary wades past a few more cops and waits for Pritchett at the bed. He arrives and takes in the gruesome sight. Michael is naked and dead on the bed. His chest is ripped to shreds and his blood has soaked through the mattress. His face is covered in slashes and his penis is split in half along its length. His knee appears to have exploded. On the ground around the bed he sees a drill, extension cord and a hot glue gun. The torture is apparent, yet the lieutenant remains stoic. After Isabella and Arpi, nothing shocks him anymore.

"He didn't die quickly did he?" He asks.

"No." Mary answers. "His knee was drilled through with a quarter inch bit, while he was alive. Causes traumatic blood loss, but not death. The slash down below his waist was also pre-mortem. Judging by the splatter patterns on the walls by the headboard, he was alive when that began as well, but he didn't last long afterwards."

"So," Jake begins, "we know that he was a pedophile, or at least someone thought he was. What about complaints against him? Have there been any?"

"HQ is has been checking the past hour," she replies, "but so far nothing has come up. He was clean as far as we can tell."

"Have someone find out where his wife is." He orders. "She's either a prime suspect, or a target. Get her in protective custody."

"She won't be cooperative." She responds.

"Why not?" He demands.

"Haven't you been listening to the wire Jake?" She asks. "Another one of her girls was killed in San Diego this afternoon."

"What?!" He shouts. "Why wasn't I informed of a homicide involving my case?"

"Because it's not a homicide." Mary answers. "She and her driver were apparently transporting a loaded weapon, unbeknownst to them. It went of when they hit a dip in the road. Purely accidental."

"Accidental my ass!" He yells back.

He turns away and storms out of the motel room. He takes out his cellular phone and begins to dial Raylene's number. He does not know if she is aware of her husband's demise, but that is not important. He needs to get her somewhere safe.

Raylene quietly sobs in the passenger seat of Ben's car. Three of her girls have been killed, and she cannot help but fear for Willow and Domi. She dialed the office line three times, but each call has been unanswered. She tries a fourth time, and to her relief. Someone answers.

"Hello?" the quiet female voice asks.

"Oh thank god you answered!" Raylene replies. "Who is this?"

"Who is this?" The voice asks back.

"This is Raylene Cordova." Raylene says. "To whom am I speaking?"

"Hello mother." The voice says coyly.

Raylene is puzzled by the tone of the speakers voice. It is soft, quiet, and feminine, but at the same time raspy and heavy; almost sinister.

"Natalie?" Raylene asks.

"Hurry back." Natalie says. "We are all waiting."

"Natalie," Raylene pleads, "Let me speak to…"

Click. the phone goes dead.

"Natalie." Raylene shouts. "Natalie! Fuck!"

She begins to dial the office again, but an incoming call interrupts her dialing. She does not recognize the number, but she answers in haste.

"Natalie?" She asks.

"Ms. Cordova." A male voice replies. "This is Lt. Pritchett. I need you to meet me at the Parker Center station ASAP, without delay."

"I can't right now." She protests.

"I'm afraid this is not open for discussion or negotiation." He responds. "You will immediately head for the Parker Center. Is that clear?"

"No." She answers. "I'm going to my office to pick up my daughter. Then I'll head to your station. Is that clear?"

"Very well." He replies. "I'll head to your office and pick you up."

"That will be fine." She says. "Goodbye Officer Pritchett."

She hangs up the phone as the car turns into the parking structure. After parking the car, she and Ben board the elevator and ascend to the 42nd floor.

Natalie has long laid her sister back down and now walks the hallways of the 42nd floor. Using her office keys, she locks all the fire escapes and the other office doors, save for the one Willow chucked her through. After the task was complete, she heads to a maintenance closet and retrieves a hammer. Afterward, she heads the far end of the hallway to wait. She takes her perch by the circuit breaker and listens. When she hears the ding of the elevator, she trips the breaker and hammers the boards, rendering it useless. Quietly, she slinks back to the room where Domi lays.

As soon as the elevator opens, Raylene quickly exits; only to freeze a second later when the lights die. A loud crashing sound at the end of the hall makes her jump and clutch her chest. Standing still, she carefully scans the hallway as the emergency lights kick on.

Ben stands behind her and scans as well. He sees an office door that appears to have been busted away from its hinge. "What happened to the power?" Raylene asks.

"I'm not sure." Ben replies. "Probably just a short. Go get Domi. I'm gonna check out this office and I'll meet you back here in a few minutes."

Raylene nods her heads and heads down the hall. The emergency generators kick in, but only faint light fills the hall. She can see only a few feet ahead of her so she moves slowly. She reaches the door of the office where she left Domi to sleep and opens it.

The room is very dark and Ray can barely get her bearings. She sees her daughter sleeping in the corner and heads over to her.

"There's my angel." Ray says softly and leans in.

Dominique does not move or respond. Raylene gets closer and nudges the child, but still gets no response.

"Domi?" Ray asks. "This is not funny. Say hello to mommy."

The girl is non-responsive. Raylene grabs her daughter by the shoulders and gives her a little shake. The girl's body moves stiffly and her heads slumps. Raylene places her hand on the girl's mouth and feels no breathe. She feels her wrist and neck, but feels no pulse.

"Domi!" Raylene yelps. "Dominique!"

She begins to sob loudly while shaking her daughter, desperate to rouse her from her slumber, but nothing she tries succeed. She cries hysterically and holds her daughter's corpse. She feels her grip on reality slip away and wants to scream; but a sudden intervention keeps her quiet.

"You missed it." A voice says.

Raylene's heads shots up and she scans the room.

"Who's there?' Ray asks tearfully.

"She slept so peacefully." The voice says.

"Help me." Raylene pleads. "Please, she's my daughter. She's all I have."

"She was all you had!" The voice shoots back.

"No!" Raylene cries. "You monster!"

"I am not a monster!" the voice shouts back. "Only judgement."

The outburst from the stranger clears Raylene's senses. She keeps the shadowy figure in her sights, while also looking for a way out of the room. This stranger is obviously the killer that's been stalking her agency.

"Please." Raylene begs. "You've taking everything me."

"Oh no." The voice interrupts. "Not everything. Not even close, but I'm getting there."

Raylene thinks she sees an opening so she makes a break for the door, only to be meet by a fist to the nose. She recoils and falls back to the floor. Holding her nose, she gets hysterical.

"What do you want from me?!" she screams.

"Nothing." The voice calmly replies. "I want nothing from you. I want to give something to you."

"Give me?" Raylene yells. "Give me what?"

"The pain I've had to live with for a lifetime." The voice answers.

Slowly, the figure steps forward and stares Raylene in the eye. Horrified, the woman locks eyes with her oldest daughter. Natalie continues to speak while Raylene stays silent.

"I'm a monster?" Natalie asks. "You birthed me, so what does that make you? A demon? You've shown me nothing but hate and malice since the day I emerged. You never wanted me, and you blamed me for your failed career."

"That's not true." Raylene pleas, causing Natalie to violently punch a nearby wall.

"Stop lying to me!" The girl screams. "All you fucking do is lie!"

Raylene is taken aback by this accusation, so Natalie continues.

"I heard you talking to Arpi; about not wanting me; not even having a name for me, and how she is the daughter you always wanted, as were other countless bitches. So I decided to find your favorites. The crackhead Izzy, the dumbass Willow, that bitch Arpi! And Hera, I kind of actually liked her but, fuck it, she had to die too."

"That was you?" Raylene asks, now fully terrified. "How could you?"

Natalie reacts. She charges her mother and pins her to the wall, holding a blade to her throat.

"How could I?" She repeats. "How could you?!"

She motions towards her dead baby sister on the floor and continues.

"You replaced me." She roars. "She was innocent in all this, but she was my replacement. Killing the others, painfully, was easy. But I loved her. Loved as much as you did, so I knew her death was hit you the hardest."

Raylene begins to lose her composure at the mentions of Domi's killing.

"At least she went peacefully, in her sleep." Natalie continues. "And at least she died, before you could allow her father to rape her."

The shock of the accusation brings Raylene back to reality. Natalie knew about Michael, but she thinks Raylene was complicit. If she had any hope of surviving this she has to defend herself.

"Please Natalie." She begs. "I would nev-"

"Shut up!" Natalie screams and presses the knife harder against her mother's throat. It doesn't slit her throat, and does dig into the top layer of skin, causing a bleeding wound.

"You knew!" She continues. "You knew what he was, what he did, what he was capable of, and you let him lie in the same home as my sister? How dare you!"

Natalie violently drops her mother and steps back. She tries to compose herself, to enjoy her moment of triumph; but talking about Michael possibly hurting Domi pushes her further over the edge.

"Fuck it." She says quietly.

She turns quickly and tries to kick her mother. Raylene has a split second to react and gets out of the way. Her daughter's foot strikes the wall, right where her head would have been. Missing her target, Natalie lunges towards and tackle her mother.

Raylene falls backwards as Natalie lands on top of her. She crosses her arms over her face, as she tries to fight the girl off of her. Natalie thrusts the knife downwards, trying to stab her mother in the chest. Raylene blocks each blow, but the blade slides across her arms, causing her blood to drip on her shirt. In a desperate move, she uses one hand to hold Natalie's stabbing arm in place, and pushes her other hand against Natalie's face. Natalie reels back and Raylene gains just enough room to squeeze out and get off the floor. She takes off out the room with Natalie in hot pursuit.

"RAY!" Ben yells as he comes around the corner.

"BEN!" Raylene yells back.

The two collide at the end of the hall. Raylene clutches to Ben as he helps her off the floor.

"What happened?" He demands.

"Help me!" Raylene pleads. "She's crazy!"

Raylene looks up at Ben. His face is wet and red. He has been crying, but there is no time for an inquiry.

"Oh mommy!" Natalie yells from the hall.

Ben and Raylene look down the hall and see Natalie approaching them, knife in hand. In a rage, Ben pulls out his gun. He points it at Natalie and his hands tremble.

"YOU FUCKING BITCH!" He roars.

"You better shoot me!" She yells.

"What the fuck did you do to Willow?!" He demands.

"Gutless." She mutters to herself.

She takes off running towards her targets. Ben does not hesitate and pulls the trigger. A loud 'POW' echoes off the walls and everyone freezes. Natalie falls to the ground and panics. She holds her abdomen and waits for her moment of death.

No effect!

That voice goes off in her head. As she clutches her stomach, she feels no warmth, no wetness, and no spread of blood. She is not shot.

Remember!

That's when it stuck her. She replaced Ben's gun with the fake earlier in the day. His gun is loaded with blanks. Laughing, she gets back to her feet.

"What the fuck?" Ben asks and fires again.

Natalie starts to walk forward, no longer reacting to the gunshots. Ben fires three more shots and Natalie runs towards them again. Ben forcefully pushes Raylene away.

"RUN!" He yells.

Raylene dashes and Ben is right behind her. Natalie lunges and wraps her arms around Ben's leg, bringing him to the floor. Taking advantage, she sinks the length of her blade into Ben's thigh. He screams in agony. Hearing this, Raylene runs towards Ben. She grabs Natalie by the hair and tries to throw her off. Natalie swings wildly with the knife and catches her mother across the abdomen. Raylene falls backwards grunting in pain.

The wound is not deep, but the blood still flows. She skirts over to the wall and leans against it. Natalie gets off the floor and scampers to her mother. Grabbing her by the neck, she prepares for a final thrust.

CRACK!

Natalie blacks out and slumps to the floor. Raylene look up and sees Ben standing on one leg, holding the muzzle of his gun. After striking Natalie with the butt end, he falls to the ground, clutching his bleeding leg. Raylene crawls over to him and they help each other up.

"Thank you." She says.

"We gotta get out of here." He replies.

He throws his arm around Raylene and together, they hobble to the elevators. Raylene pushes the call button, but it does not respond.

"Shit!" She utters. "She cuts the power."

"The fire escape." Ben suggests.

The hobble to the door of the fire escape. Ben jiggles the handle, but the door will not open. Raylene tries her key, but it will not fit.

"Dammit!" Raylene curse. "She broke her key off in the lock."

"There's another one through the back office." Ben says.

They make their way through the broken door leading to the back office. The office has been thrashed, and Ben knows why. It's the reason for his tears earlier in the evening. He wants to break the news to Raylene, but she suddenly lets go of him. He drops to the ground as she runs towards a desk in the far corner. She reaches her destination and falls to her knees, next to Willow's dead body.

"Oh, Willow my darling." She weeps.

Willow's body is badly beaten, black and blue, and a pool of drying blood rests underneath her head. Her skull has been crushed and a pen sticks jammed in her eye socket. Raylene lowers her head to cry. Ben gets up and kneels next to her. He reaches down and holds Willow's dead hand for a second. He turns back to Raylene and helps her off the ground. They continue to limp toward the fire escape.

"Private Spence come in over." Ben's radio roars to life. "Are you still on escort for Ms. Cordova?"

"Shit!" Ben yelps. "My radio!"

He frantically reaches into his belt for the radio. A brief sense of relief comes over Raylene.

"Call for help!" She says.

"I'm on it." He replies. "Dispatch, come in. This is Private Spence requesting emergen..."

DONG!

Ben flies forward as a fire extinguisher crashes into the back of his head. Raylene glances in horror and sees Natalie standing behind him. The girl rears back and swings again. She catches Raylene flush in the chest. Raylene flies backwards and the wind rushes out of her body. On the floor, she raises her groggy head. She sees Natalie standing over Ben's prone body. As he tries to recover, Natalie swings the extinguisher into his head repeatedly. Ben soon stops moving, but Natalie continues. Raylene can hear the sickening crack of his skull as each strike connects. His death is imminent. When nothing remains of his former head, Natalie turns her attention to her mother. She stops when she hears the crackle of Ben's fallen radio. She throws the extinguisher onto the radio to silence it.

Raylene tries to get up off the floor, but she cannot move fast enough. Natalie walks up and kicks her in the face. Kneeling down, Natalie grabs Raylene collar and punches her multiple time without mercy. She then picks her up, drags her to the window and throws her against it. Grabbing her by the hair, she smashes Raylene's face into the window, over and over. She smiles each time the blood splatters. After a minute or so, she drops her to the floor.

Raylene cannot move. She is dizzy and can barely breathe. She has no fight left in her and cannot possibly take anymore punishment. Natalie picks her up on final time and dumps her on a desk. The desk slides when Raylene lands on top and Natalie sees that it is on wheels. She looks at her mom for a final time.

"All you had to do," she says, "was love me. As you go to your grave, know this. I hate you!"

With those final words, she pushes the desk towards the window. The desk crashes through the window and plummets forty-two stories towards the earth, taking Raylene with it.

Lt. Pritchett is inside his squad car outside the building housing the agency. He grabs his radio to call in his situation.

"Dispatch," he says, "This is Lt. Jake Pritchett. Over."

"Lt. Pritchett we read you over." The radio responds.

"I am parked outside the twin towers in Century City." He says. "I'm picking up Raylene Cordova and I need to have her pla…"

CRASH!

BANG!

"WHAT THE FUCK?!" Pritchett yells as he ducks for cover.

The windshield and roof of his car violently caved in and his shotgun discharged. He looks up from his cover and sees the back of a woman's head breaching his shattered windshield. Warm blood ooze from the top of the car and drips on his dashboard. Pritchett jumps out of the car and surveys the damage. He cannot see the woman's face, but her body is beaten and bruised; and a gaping hole is smoking where her abdomen was; a result of the shotgun discharge. Pritchett walks to the other side of the car and sees her face.

"Jesus Christ!" He exclaims.

He runs back inside his car and radios for help.

"Dispatch," he begins, "we have a murder here; dispatch all available units to 2021 Century Park West. Suspect may still be on the premises."

He bolts from the car and heads to the entrance to the building. He withdraws his gun, as he must be ready for anything.

Looking out the 42nd floor window, Natalie sees her mother crash land on the squad car and witnesses her abdomen explode from the shotgun blast. It was more gruesome than she hoped for, but a fitting end to the wench's life.

"Goodbye mother." She says quietly. She then leaves the window and heads for the fire escape in the back of the office. The police officer is in hot pursuit and escape may be impossible. Finding the fire escape she runs as fast as she can to towards the bottom floor.

Pritchett races inside the building and calls the elevator. Upon arrival he tries to get to the 42nd floor, but the car is unresponsive. After pressing futilely a couple more times he tries all the buttons in reverse numerical order. The car responds to the 40th and begins the ascent.

Exhausted, sore, and bleeding from multiple areas, Natalie maintains full speed while sprinting down the stairs. She reaches the bottom floor and heads into the main foyer. She looks out onto the street and sees her mother's corpse slumped over the cop car. She blows it one final kiss goodbye and runs out the rear exit. Other police vehicles arrive, but Natalie is gone before a perimeter is established.

Pritchett reaches the 40th floor and uses the fire escape to reach the 42nd. He kicks the door open and is met with darkness, save for the glow of the lights from the emergency generators. He checks every door he walks put. Most are locked, others are small offices. He checks an office down the hall and finds a little girl who appears to be sleeping. After attempting to rouse her, he checks her pulse and realizes she is dead. He leaves her and continues to check the floor. Leaving the hall, he comes across a large double door that looks as if it was forced open. Peering inside, he finds more destruction as well as two more dead bodies. He gets on his radio and reports the situation.

"Dispatch, this is Lt. Jake Pritchett. I'm on the 42nd floor of 2021 Century Park West. Calling in a double, possibly triple homicide. Two Caucasian females, one in her late teens or early twenties; the other no older than eight years old. One Caucasian male, L.A.P.D. officer Benjamin Spence. Officer down, I repeat officer down."

He continues to search the floor and finds the other fire escape. The door is wide open and a trail of blood is leading down the stairs. He follows it as far down as he can, but the train dissipates after the 23rd floor.

"Pritchett, come in. This is dispatch come in." His radio blares.

"This is Pritchett." He replies.

"We have a perimeter established." The radio says. "Do you have anyone in custody?"

"Negative." He replies. "Get CSI in here. There is evidence all over the place, but the killer's not here."

Natalie has returned to her hotel room and locks the door. The deed has been done, but what now? She takes a shower and tries to get herself together. The hot water works its magic on her as usual, but she cannot rest long. She knows she has to move. The police have her name on file from that brief interview, and they may discover soon enough that she has been staying at this hotel. After her shower, she changes her clothes, packs her bags and leaves her room. She checks out of her hotel and walks down the street pulling her large bag. She is lost. She has nowhere to go, and no one to turn to. She stands in the middle of the street and just stares.

What now?

Even the voices cannot guide her. She walks for another mile and comes across a small motel. As before, she pays cash, leaves no info and checks in for a night. In the morning, she wakes and hopes for clarity, yet receives very little. She has no plan, no target, and as far as she can tell, no reason to continue.

Tuesday morning arrives, and Pritchett is still at the station, waiting for a report from Mary about all the samples collected from the scene last night. He needs something he can use to nail this killer, but has only found frustration. Mary walks in and cannot wait to give the information.

"We got something!" She exclaims.

"What is it?" He asks.

"A possible suspect." She replies. "Look at this."

She lays out her reports and her evidence and begins to explain.

"Let's go back to Apri, because that's where it begins to come together. We pulled some skin cells of the rope uses to hang her. Some of the blood and hair we got off of Willow matches those skin cells. This makes sense and lets us know that there I only one killer. The same DNA was found on the tools we found in the motel room where Michael was left. Now, when we started drawing blanks in our theories, I ran that DNA trace against all our victims, and I got a match."

"One of the victims was the killer?" Jake asks.

"No." Mary replies. "The DNA match came back as remarkably similar, but not a 100% copy. So the killer we are looking for is related to not only one, but two of the victims."

"Which two?" He asks.

"Raylene and Dominique Cordova." She answers.

"Raylene and Dom…" He cuts himself off. "The receptionist?"

"Right." She replies. "Natalie Cordova. Raylene's first daughter. I read in your notes about how she mentioned that she and her mother were alienated and she was basically disowned. That could be motive. Revenge"

"Do we have anything concrete?" He asks.

"Check this out." She grabs another stack of papers and drops them in front of Jake. "Natalie was a student at Salem West High School in Salem, Oregon. Afterwards she attended Westin State University last year. If you recall…"

"Six students were murdered there." He interrupts.

"Right." She continues. "Those students were also Salem West graduates in the same class as Natalie. As the murders were being investigated, the lead Detective Katrina Olivares notes that Natalie has a full on panic attack when confronted by three of those other students. She claims she was bullied and emotionally tortured by them her whole life. Six students, six tormentors, all dead."

"Coincidence?" He asks.

"Possibly." She goes on. "Detective Olivares could not put the pieces together because she was killed after the third victim was discovered. Afterwards, the last students were found dead at a construction site. One of them was paralyzed from the neck down and buried alive. They also have some foreign DNA from that case, so I'm waiting for them to fax me the details."

Pritchett stares forward in stunned bewilderment. Mary continues.

"One week ago in Salem, a small neighborhood complained of a foul smell coming from their neighbor's yard. That neighbor is Rebecca Delmonte Cordova, Natalie's grandmother. That house was Natalie's last registered address. Police dogs dug up a corpse in the backyard, identified as the good grandmother. Natalie is nowhere in sight. The poor woman had been decapitated. Except for the grandmother, we have Natalie on record saying she hated the other victims. She leaves Westin, the murders end. She come to Los Angeles, our nightmare begins. It's possible that Natalie is our killer, but all this evidence is not enough for a conviction."

"No it isn't," Jake replies, "but it's enough for a warrant. Let's get Judge Warren on the phone and see if we can make it happen. Do we know where Natalie is now?"

"Her activities show she checked out of the Hilton on Sepulveda last night." She says.

"Shit." He replies "I want bulletins sent to and posted at all airports, cab companies, and train stations up and down the state. We need to know where she is a keep her in the city."

"We're on it." Mary says. "If she's still in the state, we'll find her."

Tuesday morning finds Natalie remaining in a mental haze. She still has no direction and no reason to go on. She finds herself back at The Sacred Stain and is memorializing her baby sister with a tattoo on her wrist. The initials DMC surrounded by a flowery heart on her right wrist.

"All done." Kitty says as she finishes Natalie's latest ink.

"Thank you." Natalie tearfully replies and gives Kitty a big hug.

"You sure you alright hun?" Kitty asks. "You need me to get Willow in here to whip you into shape?"

"No, that's ok." Natalie says. "I just need today to myself. Hey do you have internet here?"

"Sure thing." Kitty answers. "Free of charge so help yourself. It's over by station two."

Kitty goes to the back to attend to other business. Natalie signs onto the PC and logs into the Femmes-Jolies network server. She doesn't know why, she was just curious. She checks Raylene's e-mail inbox just to be nosey. What she discovers awakes all her senses. As she reads the words of the newest email message received the previous day, she feels something she has never felt before.

Raylene,

After all these years I have finally found you, yet I feel my real search has only begun. 19 years ago, you and I shared in an experience that truly moved my heart and touched my soul. However, I soon came to realize that you were only using me to gain favor within the industry and further your career. You cared nothing about me or the future I believed we were destined to share. I know you became pregnant with our child, but instead of sharing in my joy you struck me in scorn and forever tarnished your reputation. The years have passed and you have achieved success and for this I am happy for you. I have spoken to your mother a few occasions and came to discover that you had a beautiful baby girl. Where is my daughter? I have gone on to live my life, find a wife and children of my own, however; there has always been a hole in my heart for the daughter I have never known. Even to this day I long to hold her in my arms, soothe her sorrows and let her know she is loved. My prayers are filled with the hopes of one day uniting with her and welcoming her into my heart, my home, and my family. You can avoid me no longer. By your American laws, I know that she is of legal age and deserves to know the truth, that she was taken from me before I had a chance to hold her. I will not be denied my chance. I will be in your country and your city this Tuesday and I will reclaim what is mine and you will not be able to stop me. So I ask you again, where is my daughter?

Alphonse Parrish

Natalie tearfully whispers, "Daddy…"
Hope…

www.ingramcontent.com/pod-product-compliance
Lightning Source LLC
Chambersburg PA
CBHW022049050726
47591CB00002B/458